COP LAND

Also by Mike McAlary

Good Cop, Bad Cop (1994)

Cop Shot: The Murder of Edward Byrne (1990)

Buddy Boys: When Good Cops Turn Bad (1988)

COP LAND

MIKE MCALARY

BASED ON THE SCREENPLAY
BY JAMES MANGOLD

NEW YORK

Library of Congress Cataloging-in-Publication Data
McAlary, Mike.
    Copland : based on the screenplay by James Mangold /
Mike McAlary.
— 1st ed.
        p. cm.
    ISBN 0-7868-8252-2
    I. Mangold, James.
PS3563.C2647C66   1997
813'.54—dc21   91–18699
                                                         CIP

Designed by Nancy Singer

FIRST EDITION

    10 9 8 7 6 5 4 3 2 1

COP LAND

PROLOGUE

H e wanted to be great again.

So sometimes, at night, Freddy Heflin would drive down to the Hudson River and stare at the city he could never belong to as a police officer. Once, as a young man, he had sat on this same New Jersey riverbank and dreamed of growing up blue. Now, all these damaged years later, he sat, pudgy with fate, in the dark, watching. He sat alone, with the lights from the George Washington Bridge over him like some glorious constellation. The starry blue lights, like the city they led to, were always just beyond his reach. The music of the great operas rose in his ears as he stared at the great city he could never belong to. Maybe he cried. He had done that before. He used to cry with longing and want. Now he grew teary with disappointment.

Hey, life was disappointing.

Sometimes he would remember the night when he had come here as a teenager, sat under the bridge, and stared across the water at his future. There was a badge for him in New York City. But then, as he dreamed, the green car would hit the water in front of him again, changing his destiny. Again, he struggled to get to his feet. He had been nineteen years old, filled with the strength and single-mindedness that is a young hero. He saw the bubbles rising up from the car and he dove. Every time he sees the bubbles,

1

he dives into them. Every night. Every bubble. The memory never changes. Reality, unlike dreams, is like that. You can never change what you did. And so, for as many times as he came down to the New Jersey riverbank to stare at New York City, he could not change the man he had become, or the choice he had made.

Once, when it counted, Freddy Heflin had mattered. Perhaps it had ruined him as a person, but the action had made him as a man. So he dove into the bubbles again. Once, I was a great hero, Freddy thought. I saved one life and lost my own. Will I ever be whole and capable of doing a great, brave thing again?

Freddy Heflin, now the forty-two-year-old sheriff of Garrison, New Jersey, started his patrol car. Then he put the car in reverse and retreated from the question and the swirling memory.

ONE

The bar reeked of smoldering rage and stale comradeship. Outside the Garden State, New Jersey was thought of as a greasy, malignant stain on the country. But most of the people living there knew it could be worse. It could be *The City,* as they called it. They liked not being from New York City. They only visited the place to see a Broadway show, or they took part in a rabid radio talk show over a cell phone. Their home was a success story. If you lived in the green Garden State, you had escaped an oppression. So, in most gin mills, when kids showed their New Jersey drivers' licenses to the bouncer, you checked trouble at the door.

The Four Aces Tavern was a cop's bar in a suburban cop's place. That made it a white joint. Oh, the occasional black, Hispanic, or Asian male was welcome in the Four Aces. Provided they showed their shield and PDA card at the door. And sure the cops were bigoted—they'd had the black mayor's face serving as the bull's-eye on the dartboard for years, but so long as a gentleman wore blue and an NYPD patch on his shoulder, he was ace enough for this place.

No one did drugs openly in the tavern anymore. A young lady could snort her nose off in the ladies' room, and a fellow could smoke a newspaper roll of stolen ganja in the parking lot outside the Ferry Plaza Building, but the Four Aces was not looking to become a new stomping ground for Internal Affairs. The Four Aces was not one of those cop bars the newspapers had made famous in East New York and the South Bronx a couple of years ago. In those places, cops met after a ripoff to cut up the dope and cash on the pine bar. During the height of the crack years in Brooklyn, whacked-out cops fired their guns into the ceiling and ran trains on hookers on the pool table. Then Internal Affairs moved in. In Harlem the rat patrol had set up their own after-hours bar and wired it for sight and sound. Within six months of Operation Last Call—as the police commissioner later named it—the cops were stealing stolen drugs and guns over the counter and working a team of six hookers out of the lounge. The customers were all doing federal time now, their badge numbers retired by the NYPD. So, after the drug scandals in Brooklyn's 75th precinct and Harlem's 30th precinct, uniformed cops couldn't, and didn't, want to be seen as such obvious fiends anymore. The cops who hung out at the Four Aces Tavern might glom a few dollars off a dead body, or shortchange the property clerk on vouchered guns, drugs, and cash, but these cops did not join the force to become criminals. And that decision made all the difference in dedication to the job. They still saw themselves as good guys. The only crime worse than being a thief to this gathering of guns and badges was being a cheese eater—a cop who ratted out a fellow officer, even a bad one.

The Four Aces was a dank, brooding place lined with framed newspaper stories from the *New York Post* and the *Daily News* about cops who lived and even died as heroes to the NYPD. Mostly, they were dispatches from the war being fought across the river. There was one story about a cop who beat the FBI agents to solving a terrorist bombing at Grand Central Station, and another article about two white cops gunned down by members of the Black Liberation Army on a Queens street. There was the story of a Brooklyn cop who committed suicide rather than rat out his buddies, and the story about an FBI agent who leaked information to gangsters. The headlines that were the vocabulary of cop life jumped out: "Suicide," "Acquittal," "Cop Shot," "Cop Killer," "Framed," "Convicted," "Raped," "Beheaded," "Saved," "Tortured."

Even the pinball machine was a monument to cops—a *Lethal Weapon II*—complete with flashing red lights and wailing sirens. And the only thing lower than a rat to these cops was a fireman. The centerpiece headline in the cop bar trumpeted "Firemen Arrested." The *Daily News* subhead explained: "They robbed from the dead." Indeed, the sign in the Four Aces over the ladies' room door opposite the "Real Men's Room" read HOME OF THE BRAVEST. On most nights in the Four Aces, bathroom humor prevailed.

Still, the smoky bar with the creaking silver radiators, blue-and-white tile floor, unsteady wooden tables, empty napkin holders, and PDA bumper stickers was a hard-drinking place where everyone had a curse on their lips and a chip on their shoulder. And if survival, in every police department, in every city in the world, can be reduced to an "us and them" mentality, the Four Aces was an "us" place where the street sign over the dartboard read VIGILANT ST. No regulars at the Four Aces could remember one of "them" surviving a night in the gin mill that was their gathering place in Garrison, New Jersey. There were fights in the place, but never serious ones. On the first night that the Transit cops traded in their .38-caliber Smith & Wesson specials for the 15-shot Glock 9s, two of the boys shot up some bottles on a car in the parking lot, but no one had ever fired a shot in anger inside the place. Once, a rookie accidentally fired his gun while taking a dump, but the fellow later left the NYPD to join the FDNY. He never set foot in either bathroom again. And if there was any doubt about how civilized the cop bar was, all one had to do was order a pitcher of beer. They still served swill in glass pitchers and drank it out of glass mugs in Garrison, New Jersey. The town was a civilized cop place.

An invention of the Patrolman's Development Association, the town was an impossibility, really. New York City cops are only allowed to live in the state of New York. They are only licensed to carry guns in New York. So, some of them lived in the far reaches of Suffolk and Orange counties. Once they'd even discovered a New York City cop—a bit of a thoroughbred horse fan—who lived in Saratoga, a full five-hour drive from his Staten Island precinct. By law, the only cops who worked in the city who were allowed to live in New Jersey were the Transit cops. They were employed by the Metropolitan Transit Authority—an agency controlled by politicians from New York, New Jersey, and Connecticut. So, in the beginning, the only cops who lived on the New Jersey side of the George Washington Bridge and worked in New York were Transit cops. There were some cops who started as Transit cops and then transferred into the NYPD. They were given hardship status until they were able to sell their homes.

But then one of the PDA leaders, a degenerate gambler named Dennis Hardy, who worked on Broadway in Manhattan but could only be reached during office hours at the Claridge Hotel in Atlantic City, heard about the cop gathering in Garrison, New Jersey. Hardy was the first person to learn that the city intended to merge the Housing and Transit police forces under the control of the NYPD. So before the merger went into effect, he got some of the NYPD's best and brightest young cops to transfer into the Transit force. Many made the cuts and bought homes in New Jersey just under the merger cut. When the three police forces became one, Hardy got the city to agree to grandfather in the police occupants of Garrison, New Jersey, as exceptions to the city's residency requirement. The union even got them gun carry permits in New Jersey. Of course, there could never be a New Jersey town like Garrison again after the police merger of the mid 1990s, but that was fine with the cops who lived there. The cops celebrated the ruling that allowed a team of New York City cops to live across the Hudson River at the Four Aces. They even put up a sign outside Garrison, New Jersey, in the days after the ruling. It read: IF YOU WORKED FOR THE NYPD, YOU'D BE HOME NOW. The *Post* and the *News* both loved that one, almost as much as they loved the story of the New Jersey cop who continued to patrol after he/she had undergone a male-to-female sex-change operation. You could look it up if you wanted. The framed story was hanging over an unused spittoon in the Four Aces Tavern.

TWO

Freddy Heflin was playing cop again. Near the oak bar in the Four Aces, he leaned over the *Lethal Weapon* pinball machine. Freddy was the best pinball cop in the joint. The machine said as much. The thing blinked his score every hour of every day it was plugged in. And the bar never closed. The score tallies into the millions were also recorded on strips of tape, affixed to the side of the machine. All of the high scoreboards were attributed to "Freddy," the sheriff of Garrison, New Jersey.

Freddy was dull with booze again. He leaned over the machine, his eyelids heavy. He was a slump-shouldered man even when he wasn't consumed with plastic flippers. Hell, he was wearing flip-flops. His belly hung over his belt, but he was more wilted than puffy. Once he had been toned and muscular. But that was a million pinball games ago. He was hanging ten over a sandal.

"I really got it tonight," Freddy mumbled. "No stopping me tonight."

Like a boozy stalker, he focused on a nearby table. They paid him little mind. Freddy wasn't a real cop—a New York City cop. Although most sheriffs in New Jersey had to win a county election, Garrison was a county unto itself. Heflin, who ordinarily wore a neat brown-and-white uniform with an American flag over one shoulder and a Garrison, New

Jersey, patch over the other, was given the job by a friend in the PDA. Tonight, he was just wearing a faded plaid shirt.

Still, he had a sheriff's badge. Freddy Heflin was the only sheriff in the state serving by whim, not election. Ordinarily, no one paid him any mind. He stared at the table where a hard-jawed, red-haired woman, Berta Combs, about thirty-eight, was drinking. She was attractive in a Last Call sort of way. She was sitting with a man Freddy knew. They both had the peculiar vocabulary, posture, and "Don't fuck with me" manner that said they were members of the NYPD. Civilian clothes could not camouflage their occupation.

"So I get a ten-thirteen—shots fired over the air," Berta said. She was watching Freddy watching her, curious because she knew she was five years past being considered attractive this early in the night. She could smell trouble, bomb-making equipment, from half a room away. Freddie gave her the creeps, but she continued her tale.

"So I get there . . . and there's this Armenian guy, he's from the other side, over there. Told her she's dead—that she'll be dead by morning . . . Then fires the gun and leaves."

The cop sitting with her, Gary Figgis, was about forty, and a Four Aces regular. He wasn't interested in Berta sexually, especially at this hour.

"Uh-huh," he said.

"So, he drops off this box at her apartment. The bomb squad responds and we x-ray it on-scene. But I can't see anything. So I cut out a little hole . . . And there is something in there . . ."

She reached for her drink. Freddy was staring straight at her and holding the pinball on the flipper in suspense.

"Some white fuzz—and something pink. But I can't fig-

ure out what the fuck it is. And suddenly I realize I'm looking at a tongue."

"Shit," Figs offered.

"The guy put a goat's head in there."

Figs has heard and seen worse. Still, he acted vaguely
interested. Freddy has quit the game completely and has
continued to stare at Officer Berta. He is awed, of course.
Figs grabbed an NYPD duffle bag from the seat beside the
storyteller. He checked the contents with one hand as he
began to pontificate. At his own precinct, where Figs never
tires of hearing himself talk, he sometimes reads columns
by Cal Thomas and G. Gordon Liddy aloud to his fellow officers before roll call. Most of them ignored him while they
thumbed through the sports columnists, Lupica and Mush-
nick. It is tough to discuss political ideology, Figs has argued, with a room full of Ranger fans. He has started more
than one fight by referring to cops as a softball team with
guns.

"This at the end of the twentieth century," Figs said.
"H. G. Wells—he'd roll over in his grave to think that at the
start of a new millennium—that some Iranian—"

"Armenian," Berta corrected him.

The cop zipped the bag shut and put it down beside his
chair. Dave Meggett never handled a handoff as neatly in
Giants Stadium.

". . . that some, ahem, Armenian," he continued, "would
be delivering a goat's head to the door of the woman he
loves."

"He is from a backward culture . . . ," Berta tried.

Police Officer Rush Limbaugh was off to the races now.
"We're all backward. Our machines are all modern and
shit—but our minds, Berta. Our minds are primitive."

An attractive, bosomy woman emerged from the ladies'
room. A Cuban, she was brave with cocaine. She sniffled

and drew a finger against her nose. She had a sexy body but a vacant eye, a scorpion tattoo on her right biceps. She looked like half of the people Berta Combs had arrested in Hell's Kitchen when she was working Vice in Manhattan South. To her surprise, Figs called this slut by name and invited her to sit down. *With them.* Berta sighed. She had given up Vice and seeing women made up like this to join the NYPD bomb squad.

"I want to go home," the ticking woman, Monica, whispered to Figs. "We gotta go to your place and I still gotta drive back to the city—"

His beeper sounded. Figs reached for it and read the display. Berta caught Freddy staring at her, watching her.

"Excuse me," Berta told Freddy. "Do you mind?"

And then loudly, "DO YOU MIND?"

Freddy understood the invitation to mind his own business. The pinball dropped into the gutter. Freddy searched his pocket for a quarter but came up empty. Anyway, it looked like he would take a header into the glass-topped machine.

"Hey, I'm sorry," Freddy said.

Figs leaned forward and waved a finger in the air. The tension dissolved. "It's cool, Berta," Figs said. "Freddy's good people. He's only got one good ear anyway."

They separated. Figs rose, and walked to the pay phone. Woozy with booze and dull with embarrassment, Freddy stumbled to the bar. He stood next to Figs. Monica was flipping through CDs on the jukebox as Berta smoked a cigarette, studying Freddy through the haze.

"Quiet tonight, huh, Freddy?"

"They're all at the bachelor party," Freddy said. "Across the river."

Figs hung out of the wooden phone booth and whistled into the phone as he waited for his call to be answered.

"Yeah. Whoop-de-do."

And then, into the phone, "No. No. I'll hold. What is this, Freddy? You celebrating long distance?"

Freddy was silent, numb with liquor. The barmaid, Delores, emerged from the kitchen. She took the empty glass mug from the sheriff and noticed the dollar bill in his hand.

"Don't look at me," Delores said. "The register's closed and I just put two more in the goddamn parking meter."

He began to walk off, and Delores whispered to Figs, "It's his birthday. He needs quarters. He's going for high score over there."

"Oh yeah," Figs said. "Happy birthday, Freddy. Let's see what I got." He found some change.

"So where is your new girl? Your new little deputy—Wendy?"

"Cindy. At her mom's," Freddy said. "You know, I wasn't into making a big deal. After the party in New York, my ten-year deal here."

Figs started talking into the phone and held up his hand, palm out, to Freddy. He did not want to be interrupted. Freddy blinked and then shuffled out the door in search of quarters. He saw the parking meter and smiled, thinking of himself in one drunken moment as Cool Hand Luke. Unlike Paul Newman, Sheriff Freddy Heflin had a key to the meter. He took out a large set of keys and unlocked the meter. Quarters spilled out into the cop's hand and onto his bare toes. Like the worst of the crack addicts, the sheriff knelt down to gather his spilled rocks.

Gary Figgis walked out the side door. "There are just two kinds of people in the world," he announced. "Pinball people and video game people. You, Freddy, are pinball people."

The sheriff of Garrison blinked and smiled sadly. He

was too drunk for perspective or self-awareness. There was a green-and-white squad car at the curb. The decals on the side of the car read SHERIFF—TOWN OF GARRISON. Figs opened the driver's door and beckoned to Freddy Heflin. "Come on, Wyatt Burp," Figs said. "It's bedtime, Sheriff."

THREE

They called the place Scoreboards, not because anyone cared, frankly, once they walked through the front door of the place, how any of the local sports teams were doing. In this sense the word "score" meant conquest, as in sexual conquest. And although customers had to pay through the nose for any conquest of the sexual sort, the lounge was filled on any given night with the great scoring leaders of professional baseball, basketball, and hockey. The strip joint became famous—perhaps even infamous—because only one type of person was barred from entry: photographers. And so the famous and infamous could gather to ogle and grab some of the greatest looking strippers this side of Las Vegas without having to worry about winding up on the front page of the *New York Post* the following day. Oh, sure, a misdeed or ugly grab could still get you a mention on Page Six, but without photographs, the New York City tabloids quickly moved on to other business.

Although connoisseurs of lap dances and girls who gyrate on poles for a living generally rate the strip clubs of Montreal as the best in North America, the Scoreboards establishment was considered the best topless joint in the city. Amazingly, although it regularly appeared in the newspapers as mob-controlled—and even remained open through

the occasional FBI raid—the New York City Police Department never put the place on its off-limits list.

And that was surprising. Stunning, actually, when you
realized that a couple of bouncers had been gunned down at
the front door. It was rumored that half of the team that
won the NBA championship that season had to tiptoe
around dead bodies and yellow crime-scene tape on their
way out. And although there were said to be a half-dozen
off-duty cops in various stages of undress in the place at the
time of the shooting, no police witnesses ever came forward.
The managers of the place ran a cute game with the newspapers. They only favored one fellow from the *Daily News,*
Johnny Rocko. And whenever somebody hip came into the
place—say, this year's felon or last year's Oscar winner—
the photographer would get a phone call. On cue, Rocko
would be ushered in to snap his photograph, and then just
as quickly thrown out of the place bodily, negatives intact.
On this night, the cops were in the nightclub in force. Anyone squinting through the colored light could make them
out. As one stripper slid down a pole, another gyrated on a
man's lap. A crowd of men, all of them off-duty but still
wearing NYPD T-shirts and hats, stood in the back of the
room swigging mightily from bottles of beer and scotch.
They were out of control, of course. But the rowdiness was
not without precedent. A couple of years before, in Washington, D.C., some of these same city cops had turned a national memorial service for fallen cops into a drunken
madhouse. Some slid down a hotel balcony naked. Others
fired guns and disconnected fire alarms. When the cops arrived, the off-duty cops blamed the wildness on a convention
of drunken firemen.

The guest of honor tonight was Murry Babitch, a.k.a.
Superboy. He was shit-faced and covered with confetti, a

state not much different than the condition in which he
sometimes appeared at roll call. Babitch, at thirty-two,
hadn't read a book since finishing the patrol guide in the
police academy, and was subject to a patrolman's routine
bouts of insomnia and paranoia. He was a fun drunk,
though, with a one-way mouth, cops said. Beer and scotch
passed Superboy's lips freely, but police gossip never
escaped them. Although emotional and severe, Murray
Babitch was a cop's cop—a yahoo who could be trusted. He
could not be trusted to steal, however, so corrupt cops generally had no use for him.

As he wandered through the pulsing music toward the
door, they shouted at him: "Safe home"; "Take this girl as
your partner."

"Take care, Superboy," a black cop in an NYPD jacket
said as he headed out the front door.

"All right, Russ," Superboy managed. On the way out,
he waved to a couple of other cops. They hadn't had this
much fun, and been this drunk with this many naked
women, since last summer's PDA convention in the Cats-
kills.

"Cops rule, firemen drool," he chanted on the way out.
Babitch shuffled through the lot packed with civilian and
patrol cars under the Fifty-ninth Street bridge leading to
Queens. All of the cars were marked with Patrolman's Be-
nevolent Association bumper stickers. No cop would dare
ticket one of the double- and triple-parked cars. Babitch unlocked the door to his car, a yellow Honda parked in front of
a hydrant, with an orange NYPD placard poised perfectly
on the dashboard. Suddenly he heard a dull, muffled, gag-
ging sound from the back of the lot. The cop reached into
the car and pulled a flashlight and a gun from his glove
compartment. He began to walk toward the sound, the

flashlight cocked above his ear. The gun was out, in his right hand, held at his side.

The beam discovered a red-haired cop kneeling vomiting in the bushes, his uniform shirt unbuttoned. His chin was wet. He glared into the light as Babitch noticed another cop, Frank Lagonda, standing by his side, smoking.

"Hey, guys," Babitch said. "You scared the fuck out of me."

"Hey, Superboy," Lagonda said.

"Kill the light," the cop on his knees, Jack Rucker, said.

"Straight home, fellows," Babitch said, laughing.

He sighed and moved back to his car, snapped the light off, and dropped the pistol onto the passenger seat.

He put the car into gear and rolled out onto the street.

Smash! His left-front tire had crushed a beer bottle. Murray was too drunk to notice, or hear.

"Fuck me," the cop said, apropos of nothing.

The Honda began to crawl up the ramp leading through Washington Heights and on to the George Washington Bridge. Somewhere above him a spotlight shone on the sign reading LAST EXIT IN NEW YORK. Babitch, fresh from a drunken night at Scoreboards, headed onto the ramp with his head leaning against his window. Sports scores dribbled from the radio. He did not hear them as he rolled through the last red light before the bridge.

Bang!

He had been sideswiped on the driver's door by a red car. Jolted, Babitch swerved into the opposing traffic, which was being rerouted into one lane because of midnight construction. The cop reeled and lurched, then peered out the window at the damage.

Up ahead, lit by the glow of the bridge's mercury lights,

he saw the red Mazda weaving crazily. He watched it snake once more and then punched his own gas pedal. It was instinct. He approached the car from the right lane.

He pulled up alongside the kids in the joy-riding car and heard a song by Coolio. Gangsters, indeed, Babitch decided. The enraged cop glared. He met a pair of eyes in the red Mazda. He had his badge hanging out the window.

"Police!" he screamed. "Stop. Pull over."

The kids howled with laughter and their car slashed forward. One of the kids seemed to lean over toward Babitch, waving a dark object. The kid was waving a barrel at Babitch. The cop alarm in his head went off. G-U-N.

Bam! There was a blast as his front tire blew out. Babitch ducked beneath the wheel and came up swearing.

"Shit. Fuck. Piss!"

He swerved, scraping a concrete divider. The kids had shot his tire. He picked his gun off the seat, and fired, right-handed, across his body, while hanging out the window. The red car exploded ahead of him.

"Motherfucker. Motherfucker."

He fired and fired. He squeezed off a handful of shots in quick succession. After the third or fourth shot, the Mazda's rear window shattered. It was a nice piece of shooting. The car careened wildly across the bridge. Then it struck a bridge support and bounced around in the middle of the highway.

Babitch couldn't stop. He slammed into the Mazda and his head hit the windshield. He rocked back, his nose slashed. He was bloody, and alone.

The bridge was still.

FOUR

As Freddy's patrol car came over the hill, his headlights caught a deer-crossing sign. On the other side of the river, this sign would be in the middle of Harlem, on West 125th Street. As he drove, a cassette played a Sibelius piano sonata. By the middle of the first stanza he straddled the double yellow line. His eyes left the road and he stared out, perhaps even longingly, toward the lights of northern Manhattan. The reflection of the George Washington Bridge shimmered over the churning water. The cop turned back to the road and caught the eyes of a young doe in his headlights.

"Shit."

He slammed on his brakes and jerked his wheel to the right, but suddenly realized he was heading for a ravine. Freddy jerked the wheel the other way and headed toward the brush. He finally thudded to a stop against an embankment.

The last thing the drunken sheriff heard before he passed out was the young doe rushing away to safety.

The George Washington Bridge was now the flashing center of the modern, hysterical world. Lights of every color washed over the bridge. It screamed with life and mechanical terror as fire engines, emergency vehicles, cop cars, and ambulances funneled onto the bridge. The traffic was at a standstill. Vapor lights sprayed the suspension cables. At the center of the police universe sat a red Mazda RX7. Steam rose from the hood, which was impaled on a bridge support. A pair of medics were already in the car, pushing and touching a pair of black teenagers. One medic felt for a pulse. As it was gone, he reached over and turned off the music.

Police Officer Jack Rucker, last seen on his knees outside the Scoreboards nightclub, stood over the medics, watching. The driver gurgled, his ear a sopping trench. The other kid's forehead was sprinkled across the dashboard. He was wearing his safety belt. There was an exit wound in his forehead, a barrel at his feet. The Club.

Rucker picked up a crack pipe and vials. He dropped them into a plastic NYPD evidence bag. The barrel of the pipe barely fit into the bag. The medic nudged him out of the car and pointed to its rear window, riddled with bullet holes.

"Traffic incident. What bullshit, man. Nobody said they were popped."

Rucker pushed out the remaining glass.

"I can't tell if those rounds were incoming or outgoing," Rucker said.

Another cop from the nightclub, Russell, the black one, who Murray Babitch passed on the easy out, set flares on the bridge and studied the gridlocked traffic. An older cop, this one barrel-chested, stepped from the Jersey side of the traffic, a cell phone to his ear. He wore identification clipped to his jacket: LIEUTENANT RAY DONLAN. He walked easily through the chaos and destruction. He was in control, and seemed oddly unaffected by the tragedy. He started to stroll toward Babitch, who was slumped behind his car. A detective crossed the road, listening to a squawking radio. He met Russell's eyes.

"What you are just thinking, Russell, swallow it," Detective Crasky said.

"Hey," Russell said, having made the cultural decision to be colored blue. "He saved five babies in Red Hook."

"That's right," the white detective continued. "Black babies."

Across the bridge from them, Babitch sat, his badge clipped to his shirt. There was a bandage on his severed nose, and his eyes were wet with alcohol and emotion. He gulped for air, sucking it through a cigarette. He was already back in Brooklyn, where kids in his precinct used to brag, "I'm from Bed-Stuy. Do or die."

"There's going to be one million of them holding candles. I'm going to be the poster boy for the Civilian Complaint Review Board. I'm dead. My life is fucking over. They are going to string me up, Ray—just like Tunney."

He said the cop's name and Lieutenant Ray Donlan again saw the cop hanging by his bedsheet in the Brooklyn House of Detention. The note had been folded in his top pocket.

"We ain't gonna let it go down like that," Donlan said. "I'm here this time."

"Tunney didn't even live to tell the Grand Jury," Babitch said.

"Fuck the Grand Jury," Lagonda said, almost apoplectic. "You're Superboy, right? You saved what—six black babies? That shit plays."

Detective Leo Crasky, having finished with Officer Russell, walked over. He had one ear to the squawking radio.

"The car was hot."

Donlan nodded. He was pleased with the news. It was already better than a shooting on the bridge last year, when the cops had shot a young mother, in her own car, waving a toy gun. Babitch stared through him, at the sunrise over the city.

"Three babies," he said.

Crasky, the detective in charge, held the radio. A woman's voice screeched over it.

"Miss DKNY here says there's a jurisdictional question," Crasky advised Donlan. "If it began on the bridge, it belongs to the Port Authority. If it began on the ramp, it's ours."

"On the ramp," Lagonda said.

"One at a time, please," Crasky said into his radio. And then, to Lieutenant Donlan, "I got Port Authority on another channel, the mayor's office, the Manhattan DA, press up the ying-yang. The only reason they are not here is because we have gridlock from the Cross Bronx to the Palisades."

"We're lucky," Donlan said. "We have time."

"There's no gun," Rucker reported.

"Just the barrel of a steering lock."

The lieutenant looked to the detective, who handed Rucker a set of keys.

"In my trunk," Crasky said. "In a Grand Union bag."

Babitch heard and understood immediately. They were cops, ready to protect each other.

"Ray," he tried. "You don't have to. I saw it. He pointed the fucking piece at me. I heard the shot."

But Officer Rucker was already gone, to retrieve the drop from the older detective's car.

"The kid had a bottle of malt liquor in his hand," Detective Crasky explained flatly.

"But I heard the shot—" Babitch insisted.

"Your tire blew, hotshot," said Crasky. And now his voice rose. "So listen to me. Your tire blew. You fucked up and wasted a pair of shitbags who aren't worth the hair in the crack of your ass. They pointed the Club at you. So cool it with the patty-cake morality, because without me those two stiffs will put you in a room where you will fuck your uncle Ray and everything he has built."

"Hey, hey, Detective Crasky," Ray Donlan said, raising his hands, palms up. "Go easy on the kid, Leo."

The knowing detective and the controlled lieutenant exchanged a glance. They were just checking each other. Babitch saw them, and understood. They were assuring each other that he could be trusted. What if the kid was wearing a wire and Internal Affairs had set this whole thing up as an integrity check? Stranger things had happened in Brooklyn and the Bronx. There was a videotape of a Manhattan cop robbing a stash house he had been called to check out. Internal Affairs was getting better. Sometimes it seemed they had all of copdom wired for sight and sound.

"I don't drop dimes," Babitch said. "I may be a schmuck, but I'm not a rat fuck."

"Oh yeah?" Leo Crasky said. "How much blow did you snort tonight? I heard you had a fucking brick."

"Fuck you."

"Fuck you, little boy," Crasky said. "The black van is going to be here in a minute and I haven't done shit. What I am doing for you is highly—"

"Sympathetic," Donlan said, interrupting. "And it is."

"Damned right," Crasky said. He was the kind of old-time cop who didn't agree to protect anyone without a payback promise. Ray Donlan could be his uncle, too.

"I have been standing on this bridge popping pimples," Crasky said. "But fuck it, Murray Babitch. You are Ray's nephew. You are Superboy. You saved ten black babies once. And now I caught this case. And I want a simple case because this racial shit eats you alive."

Donlan listened, then turned from Crasky to his nephew, Murray Babitch. The lieutenant seemed to be weighing something.

"If this plays the wrong way, it could eat all of us, Murray."

The kid said nothing. His face fell away to nothing as Jack Rucker walked by them carrying a crumpled brown Grand Union paper bag.

The cop was strapped in now, on a police thrill ride with no brakes.

The sheriff's car was pitched against the embankment, steaming. The front end was creased and crumpled. The driver's door was open. The concert piano, unlike Coolio on the bridge, continued to play. Another car—also marked "Town of Garrison"—pulled up. His deputy, Bill Geisler, a thoroughly harmless man, shone a hood-mounted search beam into Freddy Heflin's car.

"Freddy?"

Nothing. The deputy scanned the woods under the great bridge. He found the sheriff at the water's edge. He had discovered him here before. Freddy faced the water and the lights of the city. The water moved past slowly, hypnotically. It always ran the same, past and over Freddy Heflin. Tears ran down his cheeks.

"Freddy. It's Bill."

The sheriff wiped the tears and the blood on his sleeve. Slowly, he stood to be rescued.

The medics were still inside the crushed, bloody Mazda when Police Officer Jack Rucker approached. They did not see the bag. Detective Crasky knelt at the feet of the dead kid, and gracelessly pantomimed the finding of a gun. The discovery of a *cause* for a clearly *bad* shooting.

Delivered fresh, oiled, and warm from the Grand Union bag.

"Ooooh, baby," Rucker dared to say. "Look at that."

The Hispanic medic was not fooled or even playing the same game.

"Hey, what are you doing?" he asked.

"I found their piece," Rucker said.

The cop was red-faced. He was a very bad liar. But then, he hadn't expected to be called on this by a medic.

"Bullshit, man," the medic said. "That wasn't in there."

"Yes, it was," Rucker said. "Under the front seat. It was just sitting there."

"No it wasn't."

"Yes it was."

The cop moved to take the gun out of the car. The stunned medic bravely grabbed the gun by the barrel.

"Motherfucker," Rucker said. "Let go."

"You can't do that."

There was a struggle in the middle of the swirling, screaming chaos. The argument became obvious from the other side of the bridge. Control suddenly disappeared.

"Oh shit."

The detective and the other cops began moving toward the Mazda. They were breathless. From the other end of the bridge, they could hear the siren of the approaching boss. Panicked and tearful, Murray Babitch stepped to the railing and looked over.

"I told you guys," he said. "Fuck. Fuck. I told you guys to let it be."

The medic jerked the gun out of Rucker's hands and walked to the railing. The bravery was unnerving and silly. Rucker pulled his sidearm.

"Put the gun down."

The other medic waved to his friend. "Hector. What the fuck are you doing?"

Detective Crasky moved into the situation, too, his gun also in the air.

"Put it down, Chico," Rucker said. "Now."

"What are you going to do, cop, shoot me?"

Across the bridge, Ray Donlan heard the approaching sirens. It was time to make a move. Babitch stood at the railing, facing the water. He looked as if he might puke or jump.

"I'm going down, Uncle Ray," he screamed. "Just like Tunney. I am going down."

Ray turned and saw the approaching vehicle, his mind racing. He tossed his keys to Frank Lagonda.

"Frankie, get my car started," he yelled.

Back at the Mazda, Officer Rucker trained his gun on the medic and screamed, "PUT IT DOWN!"

If they had been alone on a South Bronx street, the cop would have killed him. And the medic, who grew up in a neighborhood where a kid was strangled by a cop for hitting his patrol car with a football, knew he was untouchable with cops from two states watching. Hector smiled spitefully and turned to toss the planted gun out and over the bridge. The cops and medics leaned over the George Washington Bridge together as the gun hit the water. There was a distant splash as the fix disappeared.

"Shit," Crasky said.

Rucker leaped at the triumphant medic. He smacked him with his pistol twice before the other medic and the cops separated them.

"Motherfuck," Crasky decided.

From the other side of the bridge, there was a ghastly scream. Ray Donlan turned to them and looked ashen, absolutely bloodless. Murray Babitch was gone.

"Oh my God," Donlan yelled. "OH MY GOD. Jesus. He JUMPED!"

They all stared down at the water.

". . . he just—jumped," the lieutenant continued.

Everyone joined him at the railing, including the medic and Rucker.

"He hit the water—and he went down," Donlan explained.

Two hundred feet below them, the Hudson River churned greasy, raven and hushed. It was just another passing secret.

FIVE

The white picket fence needed a paint job. The sun sliced the floral curtains of his bedroom. If one walked to the window of the suburban house, one could see overhead the impossible monstrosity that was the George Washington Bridge. The neighborhood was oddly silent in the shadow of the bridge. The cars were honking. Screeching and braking to a new morning in New York City and yet, here, one thousand feet below the rush, it was dead silent. At this distance not even the river made a sound.

Freddy Heflin awoke with a colossal hangover. The room was quiet until he moved his head off the pillow and exposed his good ear to the alarm. He remembered something from the night before, but when he tried to grab hold of the idea, it disappeared in an earthquake of pain. He drew his hand to his nose, almost absently, and felt the bandage. Then he remembered a version of the previous evening's crash.

The birds were singing, chirping magnificently. It was going to be a beautiful day on both sides of the river.

"Fucking birds," Freddy mumbled, putting a beefy hand to his good ear. "Fucking birds wake me up."

Freddy sat on the edge of the bed and twirled his gun like a kid playing western gunslinger. He padded out of bed and walked to the window. On the porch of the house next door to him, a young man with an NYPD bag kissed his wife good-bye. A car full of men was waiting for him. It was the car pool from hell, cops making a straight run from their homes in Garrison to a set of Bronx and Manhattan police precincts.

Freddy lived in a cluttered place. He looked back at his own bed and saw what had been a fistful of quarters. There was a box of Band-Aids on the nightstand and a couple of cop thrillers by Joseph Wambaugh. Freddy Heflin was an old centurion. There was a piano in the middle of the room, classical sheet music on it.

Freddy was startled to hear the front-door buzzer, if only because he hadn't heard a car roll into his driveway. But that was not too disconcerting, Freddy missed a lot of sounds now. He was standing at his turntable, already loading an album for his good ear, when the bell sounded. Freddy still played records. He enjoyed the ancient sound of the piano better as it tinkled, even hauntingly, over the tube amplifier. Yellowed classical record albums were scattered throughout the room. Most of them featured a bent-eared pianist, Glenn Gould.

His deputy, Bill Geisler, the harmless man, stood at the door. Freddy was wearing a robe and smoking when the deputy walked into the house. He was carrying the newspapers and a grocery bag. In the morning light, his gray uniform looked as perfect as anything Robert E. Lee had ever worn. He poured them both a bowl of Wheaties.

"How long's the car gonna take?"

"Lenny won't know, boss, till the parts guy comes in. Take number two, ya told Cindy you would teach her radar today."

Freddy nodded at his deputy. Radar was their real police work.

"What did you tell Lenny—about my accident?"

"Chasing a speeder," Bill mumbled over his Wheaties. The sheriff touched his good ear. It was a practiced move. "Excuse me?"

"SHERIFF WAS CHASING A SPEEDER," Bill repeated.

The chief smiled at the lie. He had long since outgrown the point at which a man is embarrassed to admit his weakness.

"How's the nose?" the deputy continued. He tried not to stare.

"Fine."

Once Freddy had been the hero of Garrison, New Jersey, population 1,280. He had marched down the main street as the homecoming king. He was a punishing fullback then, the first great football player from Garrison High School. He wore a black eye patch before the games and rushed for 600 yards during his senior year. The great, gray, Garrison Raiders were winless during Freddy's freshman year, and the laughingstock of their conference the next year. Garrison was as empty as the water tank towering over the town. But then the PDA arrived, with all their satin jackets, score books, and coaches. By Freddy's senior year, the Garrison Raiders were state champs in their class. You could have replaced the Garrison tower with a gun turret that year. They embarrassed the Sparta Warriors in the championship game, just sent them scurrying for cover.

But within two years, following the trouble in the river, the same kid who had jokingly worn an eye patch over a perfectly good eye really was deaf in one ear. Freddy was sometimes heard to argue in the Four Aces Tavern that you could hear plenty well enough if you knew what people were secretly thinking.

On the morning after, as the birds railed against the sunshine, Bill Geisler allowed himself a good, long stare at

Freddy Heflin. The deputy was in awe of the older man, and thinking of asking his sheriff more about the accident the previous night. But Freddy avoided his eyes. This, too, was a practiced maneuver. Freddy gazed vaguely at the breakfast table and then focused on the morning copy of the *Daily News*. The story had barely made the last-edition paper. It was a fantastic tale and the editor had happily replated the front page at two in the morning, shouting at the city desk, "Finally, a race story with legs." He had settled on the headline: "Hero Cop Takes Plunge, Shoots Teens, Jumps off GW Bridge." There was a police identification mug shot of Police Officer Murray Babitch inset against a still shot of the George Washington Bridge. Inside, the *Daily News* had managed to get a studio shot of one of the black teenagers killed on the bridge. The photos of the unsmiling white cop and his vibrant young black victim were incendiary. Even Freddy, in New Jersey—half a world away from the racial Duraflame that is New York City on a calm day—could smell the gasoline bombs.

Freddy sucked on a cigarette, reading intensely. There wasn't going to be any homecoming parade in Garrison this year, the sheriff realized.

"On the way over I heard it on the radio," the deputy said excitedly. "Even Imus was pissed off. Said they was unarmed. Crown Heights *and* Washington Heights are gonna explode this time. . . ."

A woman walked to the window overlooking Broadway, in lower Manhattan. She could see right down Rector Street and straight across the Hudson River to New Jersey. She didn't actually know the name of the New Jersey town she was staring at but imagined it was Hoboken. The young woman lived in Deer Park, on Long Island, herself; all of New Jersey was Hoboken to her Long Island way of think-

ing. A handsome man in a double-breasted suit from the
$1,500 floor at Barney's—the PDA president, Vince Las-
saro—entered the room. The aide turned from the window
and scurried across the conference room to hand Lassaro a
one-page biography of Police Officer Murray Babitch, dead
in the line of duty. The police union officials were standing
outside a press briefing room and were fully prepared to
spin the story for the entire city.

"No wife," the aide said breathlessly. "He was from Jersey City."

Lassaro listened, absorbed, and then nodded toward the
still locked press room door.

"And he's Ray's nephew, right?" Lassaro said. "So put
the service in Garrison. And I want a full captain's funeral.
I want bagpipes, motorcycles, a riderless horse, helicopters—our best funeral show. Ray Donlan owns the locals.
Have him get me the seating plan. And keep the mayor's
friend—that schmuck car dealer from Queens—out of the
front row. What do these contributors think, you can buy
honor? Fuck them, and His Honor. We got a dead hero cop
here."

"You know, Vince," the aid said. "It might be a good
thing that this hero kid jumped. Two black kids, unarmed—it could have played a whole 'nother way."

The remark lit a fuse in the PDA president's head. He
did not need to be handed a written movie script to recognize a story line.

"Let's go," PDA president Lassaro said.

They had to strut through a set of PDA security guards
to reach the stage. All of the union officials were of a type.
To a man, they were almost always mustachioed. For a
while there, only city firemen had worn facial hair, but the
cops had quickly reclaimed the habit. All of the PDA types

were also coiffured, and most were manicured. There's a saying on the street that you can always tell a cop, even an undercover, by his shoes. They're always just slightly off—say, black Converse in the first year of Nike. Or Timberland boots in the Doc Martin decade. They say Frank Serpico, for example, wore Earth Shoes. Only another cop would be fooled by such footwear. PDA officials were given to black and brown loafers with gargantuan tassels. The FBI joked that the bells were big enough to hide listening devices. Vince Lassaro, PDA president, had never worked a sidewalk beat or ridden in a patrol-sector car. His shoes were as perfect as his language, bearing, and delivery.

"Murray Babitch was a hero cop," the president shouted over the reporters. "He deserved a fair hearing. But *he knew* this would not happen. Not in this city. Not under this mayor."

Lassaro paused a full beat for effect, then dropped his prepared statement. He was the perfect actor. Bigger than stage and direction.

"You know," the police union leader said, dropping his voice to feign perspective and honor. "We all learned from the tragedy of Police Officer Glenn Tunney that there is no justice for cops in this city. . . ."

On the cell phone, the reporter yelled, "No, I'm talking about today's cop. The jumper. Babitch. He pulled some kids from a fire last year. I think it was in Red Hook. Get the library on it."

One beefy white cop looked straight ahead and pretended not to be listening.

"Three black babies," the poker-faced cop said.

"I think they were black kids," the reporter parroted knowingly.

By the time Lassaro announced the funeral arrangements, the reporters were diseased. This story was one part political war and one part race war. It was the perfect news event, the kind that would piss every reader off on every side of the voting spectrum. There are no new stories in New York, most good reporters know. You just have to know which old tale the new story duplicates.

And now the reporter was thinking as fast as the PDA president. The why of this story was clear.

"They say this guy jumped because of the Tunney thing. So tell Myra, she was on Tunney, right? We need a recap of Glenn Tunney—the cop from two years ago. He shot a kid while going up a stairwell in the Edenwald Houses, remember? He shot a ten-year-old who pointed a water gun at him. He was lynched in his cell while waiting for a Grand Jury. Have her do it today. I think these guys lived in the same town. They were friends. Have her do it now. Who cares about school asbestos? Get Myra off that. This story is live— all the way live."

By comparison with the reporters' excitement, the police union president seemed tame, even lame.

"The suicide rate is a direct result of a hostile bureaucracy, a hostile public, and a hostile press. Cops have rights, too."

By then the reporters were off. The story had moved across the Associated Press wire even before President Lassaro returned to his office.

SIX

No member of the service was allowed to get off on the thirteenth floor of One Police Plaza, the headquarters of Internal Affairs. For decades the cop watchers kept their headquarters on Poplar Street, in Brooklyn. The idea was to keep all of the players hidden from each other. But then Internal Affairs got better and brighter. Police officers were told to suspect every other cop they met of working for the Rat Patrol. Once the blue wall of silence began to tumble, after yet another mayoral commission investigating police corruption by yet another judge, the new police commissioner decided to move IA right into One Police Plaza.

The rats were mainstream now, with one small exception. No ordinary cop could reach their office without an invitation. The floor even had its own secret elevator. When a visitor walked in the front door, he was hustled to a back elevator. Word of people waiting for the Internal Affairs elevator tore through the building. So, just to keep cops guessing about who was a cooperating witness and who wasn't, Internal Affairs closed the main elevators for a few hours a week and made every cop ride Chucky Cheese—as the elevator was nicknamed—to piss the whole department off. Every visitor to the building had to wear a floor-pass sticker on his lapel. The joke was that IA visitors were given passes to floors they never visited just to further confuse the watchers.

On the morning after the hysterical event on top of the George Washington Bridge, the brave young Hispanic medic, Hector Gonzalez, sat in the IA waiting room. This guy was already a hero on the black and Latin radio stations. He was rumored to be the guy who caught the white cops planting a gun on the black kids. WLIB—the city's black superstation—was raising a reward for him.

He was scared now, and uneasy in the face of officialdom. He pulled on a cigarette and pushed a phone aside. The other medic from the bridge the night before, the rational one, sat silently beside him. Detective Leo Crasky walked past Hector and held the medic with a hard examination. If looks could kill, Hector wouldn't be needing an elevator to reach the ground. The sign on the door behind him read: OFFICE OF SPECIAL SERVICES—INTERNAL AFFAIRS.

"No way that guy jumped," Hector said again. "No way."

The interrogation room was a boring set. By design, the wooden chair in the middle of the room never sat level. The table was equally cockeyed. The ashtray was always full and the pencils on the table always purposely broken. The place was designed to piss off a visitor. Comfortable cops didn't confess any faster to crimes than comfortable civilians. Internal Affairs stacked the deck.

They sat on one side of the table. The subject cop sat on the other side, while a Sony tape recorder was set on the table between them. Only the cops Internal Affairs liked, or wanted to work with, were even allowed to invite lawyers into the room. If an Internal Affairs supervisor ordered you to speak—they called it General Order 15—you were required to answer any and every question they asked. Once a cop refused he could be immediately put under suspension. The Bill of Rights did not really protect civilians once they took an oath to protect and serve the City of New York. The first guy in the box was the black cop, Russell. He was invited to talk and bring a lawyer, a PDA attorney. The Internal Affairs investigator, a black detective, Sam Carson, sat on the edge of the table with a yellow steno pad. He looked up at the window and saw a green-eyed white man measuring the players in the interrogation room. He was wearing a white shirt with the sleeves rolled up. He wasn't wearing any identification. But his silent command of the orchestrated stage told the lawyer and his client that he was in charge. He was Moe Tilden, an Internal Affairs lieutenant and police icon. Uncle Moe, as scared cops called him, was as big a legend as any cop killer they talked about in precinct locker rooms across the city. During his ten-year stay in IA, the lieutenant had led a bus caravan of dirty cops off in handcuffs. On one occasion a cop who spotted Tilden outside his Westchester home had immediately shot himself. His stings were legendary. He had set up coke dens, whorehouses, and even a sporting goods store to capture crooked cops. Internal Affairs Lieutenant Moe Tilden was not to be trifled with.

His work was fabled. He broke open the infamous 77th precinct corruption case in the mid 1980s. The case was important because crack changed police corruption in New York City. Before crack, Internal Affairs only had to worry about detectives and police undercovers in elite narcotics units stealing drugs and cash. Cops had to be around drugs to be tempted. Crack changed all that. The little rocks were available on every corner in every charred urban neighborhood. Now, every uniformed cop had to make the decision—Am I with us or them?

The worst of the corrupt suspects in Brooklyn were two

partners working the midnight shift in the heart of Crown Heights. These guys careened from crack house to crack house, holding them up. In one place they even exchanged crack vials for crumpled dollar bills. By the time Tilden heard about them, the cops were running out of bad guys to steal from in their sector. And the cops seemed to have stopped knocking off drug dealers once they'd gotten a whiff of an Internal Affairs tail. They seemed to have stopped stealing altogether.

But Moe Tilden, the professor of corruption, did not believe that corrupt cops ever went back. Once cops became meat eaters, he told his men, they never went back to being vegetarians. The trap would have to be as ruthless as the dirty cops, Lieutenant Tilden argued.

One night, responding to a call of a burglary in progress, the cops who were suspected of being thieves arrived at an apartment on Prospect Place, in the 77th precinct. The cops called the 77th precinct The Alamo. The precinct was filled with white cops who rode in from the Long Island suburbs and spent their days as an army of occupation in the heart of the city's biggest ghetto—Bedford-Stuyvesant. These mopes were met by an old lady at the door to her burglarized apartment. Shaking, the victim explained to the cops that she had come home to find her door ajar and jewelry missing from her bedroom bureau. The cops were quickly bored with the old woman's tragedy and tears.

"I ran out of the apartment," she explained. "I was scared the burglar might still be in there. I think he got it all, but I'm not sure."

The younger cop's eyes brightened. This was a half-charred tenement in the heart of what the politicians now referred to as "Black Brooklyn." No cop on patrol in the precinct cared squat about crime or an old lady's push-in burglary. Some of the raiders were screeching through the precinct with ladders they borrowed from the local firehouse at night just to break into second-story crack dens.

The older cop started to itch with boredom. But the younger one was interested.

"What do you mean, you think he got it all?"

"Well, I keep a lot of money in the closet, but I didn't dare open it," the woman explained. "The money is in a tin box under my Sunday hatboxes. Could you go in and check to see if it's still there?"

Now the older cop was enthralled by the mystery, too. He nodded to his younger partner and placed a reassuring hand on the woman's shoulder.

"I'll stay here with her," he said, pulling his pistol. "Just to keep her safe. You go in and check."

The younger cop entered the apartment, walked right over to the closet, and found the tin box under an old hatbox. He opened it and removed $200 in fives, tens, and twenties. The low denominations spoke of the woman's poverty and pain. He put the money in his pocket and then walked to the door.

"Yep," he announced. "They got it all, lady."

As the lady began to wail, the younger cop winked at the older cop. Later, they would split the money in the patrol car.

They left. After a few minutes Moe Tilden, still a sergeant, walked out of the apartment with the old lady. She was holding a wig in one hand and a videotape in the other. The film crew came out a moment later.

"No, we got it all," Moe Tilden announced after videotaping the sting.

Confronted with the movie, the cops quickly turned. They took down the whole precinct and most of Brooklyn North patrol. Operation Grandma Moses was the biggest thing to happen to Internal Affairs since Serpico. All the rest of the cop scandals in the NYPD were but variations on the same theme—uniformed cops stealing drugs and money. When the crack epidemic died in the early 1990s, so did the simple version of police corruption. It became more organized again. You needed several supervisors to get around being dirty, and maybe some help from the corrupt police union. But, hell, a corrupt cop could steal a whole town if he could get his hands on one.

So, in the same room where Tilden had once played the Grandma Moses videotapes for two corrupt cops—one of whom had soiled himself as soon as he'd heard the tape with himself asking the pathetic old lady, "What do you mean, they got it all?"—the Internal Affairs detective, Carson, opened his notebook and said to Officer Russell, in an almost bored, matter-of-fact tone, "On your way home from the strip bar—at 0200—you get this call on your cell phone saying something happened to Superboy on the bridge. And you should get over there to assist."

"Exactly," Russell said.

"And you went."

"Yes."

"Along with how many other officers?" Russell's mouthpiece added.

"But you don't know who called you," the detective continued.

The lawyer put his hand on Russell, stopping him. "Wait a minute," the PDA lawyer said, "I object. We went through this and this officer has been up all night. How many times do we need to go through it? Remember, there was a tragedy on that bridge last night."

Facing the window, unseen by the men behind him, Tilden scowled and mouthed the word "Trag-e-dy."

"My guy has already stated that he has no recollection of the phone call—"

"Your objection is noted, counselor," Carson said. "I know you want a recess. I know you are tired. But I need a better answer."

"My client—my guy—at his administrative peril has already admitted he was drinking excessively and unfit for duty . . ."

Moe Tilden whirled, his eyes bright to the attack. He seemed a man poised with a hammer.

"*We know your guy was drunk, Counselor.* The officer was drunk."

And now Tilden turned on the cop.

"You were drunk. So why then—Officer Russell, drunk as you were—did you respond to a call to duty, over your car phone, from a stranger at two A.M.?"

"I don't know. I heard Officer Babitch had an accident—and the impulse to help another cop made me go."

"Didn't you take this occasion to wonder why the response was not being coordinated over the department radio by sober on-duty officers?" the lieutenant continued.

"No. No I did not."

"You did not."

"No."

"You are going to have to give me a better answer than that, Officer Russell. You know that. You know your job is in jeopardy. You are going to have to give me a better answer than that."

"I didn't take the time to see how it was being coordinated, no . . ."

A dull, uncomfortable silence filled the room. Carson looked to Tilden, who backed off. The Internal Affairs investigators were playing good cop/bad cop with the easiest prey in that kind of situation—a fellow cop. Internal Affairs cops were always amazed by the propensity of even the most hardened street cops to confess. They all knew better. But few cops could shut up. Traditionally, this was the way Internal Affairs worked. As long as there were cops and police pensions, there would be rats and order in the police department. Carson crossed to Officer Russell.

"Have you ever been to Garrison, New Jersey, Officer?" Carson asked, apropos of nothing.

"That is another question entirely," the PDA lawyer stammered.

"Excuse me, Officer. Have you ever been to Garrison, New Jersey?"

"I don't understand what this has to do with your investigation," the mouthpiece said.

"*Counselor,*" Carson shouted. He turned to face Russell. "Would you consider the cops on the bridge to be your friends? Are these white boys from Jersey your friends, bro? You looking for a summer home in Jersey, too?"

The attorney felt some power, now. Carson was holding a fishing pole. "Oh, come on, Detective Carson. I object. This is outrageous."

"Or do those white boys *scare you?* Is that it? Does Ray Donlan scare you?"

The session eroded to shouting, as Tilden had expected it might. He reached over them and snapped off the tape recorder.

"All right, I'm gonna call a recess. Listen, Counselor. I am gonna tell you right now. If he doesn't answer our questions, he's gonna be out of a fuckin' job, okay? Pure and simple. Who does he think he's talking to—a bunch of fucking morons? Huh? Are we morons?"

It was not a question. He turned to Russell. "What the fuck is the matter with you?"

"All I'm saying is that I believe—" the lawyer tried.

"Shut the fuck up. Listen to me, Counselor. The PDA may pay your fucking bills—and they don't want this thing spreading—fine. But your guy—your client—is about to lose his job. So if he wants to save his fucking ass, he better tell us what we want to know. *Because we know anyway.* You hear me? Now you can think about it. We will give you time to think about it—like, about five minutes."

"I think we need a recess, Lieutenant."

"I'll decide when we have a recess. Not you, Counselor. Not you, Officer."

Tilden stormed past them and out of the interrogation room and toward the war room. He passed Hector on his way.

"Hey," the medic said. "Are we gonna talk or what? I want to talk to you."

"When your lawyer gets here."

He continued into the war room and the detectives stiffened. There was a maze of desks. Each cop moved out of the lieutenant's way.

"You call EMS about this guy's reputation?" Tilden yelled.

"He's the real deal," one cop replied.

One detective stood up and approached the boss. They were friends. Although deferential, this detective didn't address Lieutenant Tilden by his rank.

"Moe," he said. "Harbor. They found one of Superboy's shoes."

Tilden snorted at this news. It was the sound of a disbeliever. Carson poked his head into the office and announced, "Rucker is coming in at nine tomorrow."

"What about Donlan?" Tilden snapped.

"Next week. The PDA says he's too shook up. They say Donlan is grieving for his nephew."

Tilden asked for the name of Donlan's lawyer. He was a major piece of shit in the union, a big gun.

The boss crossed to a map and stared. There was a Chinese cocktail umbrella pinned like a water tower over the town of Garrison, New Jersey.

"I don't know," Carson said. "If Superboy is alive, he's the fucking plague, right? Why bring him home with you? I mean, *you don't shit where you eat,* right?"

Tilden turned to face his squad. His green eyes were as bright as traffic signal lights. They said, "go" to the room. Uncle Moe spoke quietly, his jaws barely moving. Smoke rose like a curse from his lips.

"But I do, Carson," Tilden said. *"I live in a house—and I eat in it. I shit and eat where I live."*

He turned to the map and thumbed his nifty red umbrella further into Garrison, New Jersey.

SEVEN

The Garrison patrol car was parked by the side of the road, just beyond the curve. It wasn't hidden. Not many people knew it, but it was an illegal radar trap. Despite what you saw in the movies, cops couldn't hide behind billboards anymore. The law was pretty clear on that in most states now. Cops had to hide in plain sight. In marked patrol cars. Some states had even outlawed undercover police units. Perhaps soon there would be no sneaking up on speeders at all.

In some counties the police tracked speeders by plane and helicopter. But in Garrison, they still caught speeders the old-fashioned way. You just pointed the radar gun and fired. That way, the local cops learned, there could be no accident.

Sheriff Freddy Heflin opened his puffy eyes and looked down as a female hand withdrew from his abundant thigh. Deputy Cindy Betts cupped her newly freed hand over a radar display as a Toyota sped past. She clocked them at 45 m.p.h. The number was green and permanent on the display. Permanent, like the yellow school zone warning a half mile down the road. That sign read 35 M.P.H. Officer Betts beamed. She had a round face and bright eyes. She wore her brown hair in a ponytail and had brown eyes that matched her uniform pants. She wore a simple Casio watch on her left wrist and carried two pens in her right shirt pocket, below the gold star. In an effort to be taken seriously, she wore no jewelry or nail polish. The uniform was baggy on her, but Officer Betts was attractive despite it.

Cindy looked at the sheriff expectantly. It was very hard to say no to the enthusiasm of Officer Betts no matter what she held in her hand. But Freddy just shook his head, watching the car fade.

"It's Gratto," Freddy said.

"Come on, Freddy. This whole town is cops. We gotta pull someone over."

Freddy winced as he pressed the gauze tape to his nose. He did not feel inclined to work, especially today.

"Why?" he asked.

Cindy Betts was like most young cops, full of determination. She still imagined that she could make a difference in the world. This kind of enthusiasm is not easily muted. The young cop sighed against the world. She was thick in the arm but not muscled or unpleasant to look at. Freddy was looking, too, envying the radar gun, as a blue Olds Delta 88 flew past them. The radar registered a fast ball at seventy-two miles an hour. Cindy glared at Freddy.

"Now you got a live one," Freddy announced. He did not know the car. More important, he did not see the PDA decal above the New York plate. The car shot along Route 36. Jack Rucker was riding shotgun in the recorder seat, as cops who carried real shotguns called it. He sprayed some Dristan in his nose. Ray Donlan, the driver, was surprised to see the Garrison patrol car parked on the bend. He had not known Freddy Heflin's crew to hide so well. He checked the rear-view mirror as he flew past the car. A third man was laid across the backseat. He was missing one shoe. Rucker played with the air-conditioning. He turned, to discover the lieutenant glaring at him.

"Ray, I'm burning up here," Rucker explained.

Red lights interrupted their conversation. The Garrison squad car was full now in Donlan's rearview mirror.

"Oh fuck this," Donlan said.

The man in the back, startled and sitting up slightly, said, "What? What?" He was frantic, but Rucker just turned and smiled at him.

"Don't freak. It's our munchkins."

Donlan pulled the Olds over to the shoulder and waited. He watched Cindy Betts climb awkwardly out of the patrol car. She was all black belt and hat as she shuffled clumsily toward her capture. The gun looked huge on her. So did a set of keys. She stood at the door and put her hands on her hips. Only then did Ray Donlan roll down his car window.

"Turn off the car, please," Betts said. It was not a question.

"I got the air on," Donlan said. He just glowered at her, sweaty and red-eyed. He was a mile from his home—on the one-yard line as it were—and about to fumble. Donlan was not a stupid man. He pushed his wallet and badge at the zealous town cop. Cindy had never seen an NYPD lieutenant's shield before. It was more gold than she had imagined. With a thin line of NYPD blue.

"You were on the job?" she asked.

Donlan was controlled and patient. But just then Rucker leaned over from the passenger seat.

"No—we're coming from Forest Hills, honey. I'm John McEnroe. This is Jimmy Connors. And that's Boris Becker in the backseat."

Cindy Betts was not scared yet. She had them dead to rights. And she was equally dead to *bullshit* cop comradeship. She took the wallet from Lieutenant Donlan.

"Is your license in here? Can you pull it out for me?"

The lieutenant strained to see if anyone was with the

young cop. It wasn't like the sheriff to let them out alone. Accidents could happen. An accident *was* happening. Still, Donlan did not get cute and overbearing.

"Oh, Christ," Rucker said.

Cindy was defeated as soon as she saw Donlan's home address: Garrison, New Jersey. She handed the wallet back to him.

"You know, this is a school zone . . ."

Donlan heard the sound of uncertainty. He read her name tag.

"Listen Miss . . . Betts. You are new, right?"

"New here. But not new on the job. I was a municipal deputy in Elmira."

Beautiful, Donlan thought. I got stopped by a walking, talking police resumé. But just then he saw the sheriff. Still sitting in the patrol car.

"Freddy!" Donlan yelled. "FREDDY!"

The sheriff climbed out of his car, and approached his neighbor, embarrassed.

"See, honey, in Garrison—when the car you're gonna tag has got a PDA sticker—I'd advise you to think to yourself, Hey, that's one of the good guys, I think I'll go catch me a bad guy."

The man in the backseat pulled at the lieutenant's shirt collar; he was nervous.

"Christ, Ray, don't make a scene."

"Sir," Cindy said, "if we let every police officer go by, there might not be a single violation in this town."

"Fine by me," the lieutenant said.

"The problem in this town ain't the people that live here," Rucker interrupted. "It's the element that visits."

From the other side of the car, Freddy leaned into the window. He studied Donlan and Rucker for a moment and then focused on the man in the back, still partially obscured.

"New car, Ray," Freddy said. "It's nice. I didn't recognize it."

"Come on, Freddy," Rucker said. "I want to go home. Tell your cupcake to heel."

"Listen, buddy," Cindy shot out. "I'm not—"

Freddy shook his head at his deputy. She was going to be a good cop. She could control her rage. Even Donlan was half-impressed with her control.

"Take care, guys," Freddy said. "I'll see you later."

Donlan saluted the town sheriff. He was doing the job he was hired to do, which was nothing at all when it came to New York City cops.

"Hey," Donlan said, pointing to Freddy's nose. "What happened to you?"

Freddy smiled, half embarrassed. Donlan didn't miss much, even in the most stressful situation. Once before he'd gotten ruined in the police scandals in the mid-1980s. In one Brooklyn precinct, Ray Donlan was on his way to being a great boss. But then police corruption and the attendant union shit had destroyed him. He had survived the scandal a flawed man.

"Oh, just a little ole fender bender," Freddy replied.

The Oldsmobile lurched away and, as it did, Freddy got a better look at the man in the backseat, who stared out at the sheriff through the rear window. He wore a bandage on his nose, too. They were mirror images of each other. Only Freddy had never seen this face in the mirror before. He had seen it on the front page of the *Daily News* for the first time that morning. It was Murray Babitch, Superboy.

EIGHT

Before New Jersey cut back on money for medicine, the county built a small brick building on Main Street for medical offices. But the doctors never moved into the Public Works Building. The cops did. Shortly after the town was invented—make that established—but well before a New York City police union became the village government, Garrison had a lonely police outpost.

Now, whenever Freddy and his two deputies left the Public Works Building to make their rounds, they hung a little movable clock on the front door. BE BACK IN 10 MINUTES.

This office used to belong to the county deputy. But ten years ago, when cops first settled here in "summer" homes, Freddy Heflin was selected as the town sheriff. His oak desk was not much to look at. He had a single lamp and a tiny American flag within reach of a gun ashtray. There was a tiny bronze statue of a state trooper and a set of rifle cabinets against the walls. In the country, unlike the city, there is no gnawing rivalry between the police and fire departments. So Freddy Heflin was not embarrassed to have a tiny red engine on his windowsill.

There was paperwork on his desk, some of it a year old and all of it useless. He kept a case of classical music cassettes near his desk. The tapes were the only things approaching important history in the room. Freddy smoked too much. Like drinking, it came with the boredom. He also liked his friends too much. Photos from the one-hour lab were scattered across his desk. The scattered snapshots had all been taken at the same party. The banner at the center of one telling photo read, "Sheriff Freddy—TEN YEARS STRONG." There was a photo of Ray Donlan with his arm around Freddy, both holding water pistols to each other's heads.

The sheriff—beer in one hand and a Carlton cigarette on his lips—looked a couple of years past strong, actually. Freddy was just a little paunchy. The baggy uniform he wore was a lie. In the city, cops called their uniforms "bags": "I was in the bag fifteen years before I got a gold shield," they would say. Or, "They took my undercover assignment away and bounced me back into the bag." In Garrison, the bag was camouflage.

Sure, the tone in Freddy's biceps, forearms, and legs was still considerable, but the sight of him in a short-sleeved shirt no longer intimidated anyone. And as Freddy's body had lost definition, his life was losing its structure.

Freddy had been married once, sort of. The justice of the peace who married them was from Jersey City. He was in jail now, along with the town's mayor and its police chief. The judge wasn't a real lawyer. All of his work was voided upon his conviction for taking kickbacks. The mayor, an Irish-born fellow, wasn't a United States citizen. The police chief, it turned out, was wanted for murder in Montana.

The girl Freddy "married," Melanie, moved to town after high school. She was a dark and mysterious woman. Their sex was passionless and pained. Later no one could ever remember them holding hands. Freddy did not understand where the girl he'd fallen in love with had disappeared to. In one moment life had been one long, glorious, country hayride. In the next moment, he was alone, rolling around in a battered pickup truck.

His wife liked Freddy's high-school friends, particularly every one of his old girlfriends. And then one morning, Freddy's wife was gone. No one ever talked about it in public, but everyone knew the gossip. Freddy Heflin, town football star, lost his girl to the town cheerleader. No one seemed to know whether this was actually true. But the petty gossip outlasted most of the town's other marriages.

So, Freddy Heflin's brooding, determined silence was somewhat understandable. Though he had no limp or disfigurement, Freddy Heflin was the town victim. Or so people said behind his back when he trudged past them on Main Street.

Freddy Heflin was sitting at his desk, reading the *Daily News* and the *New York Post* for the third or fourth time that morning, studying the picture of the suicidal cop, when Cindy Betts burst into the office. The sheriff put a hand on the cop's photo.

"How do I know that guy?" she asked. Cindy was a good enough cop for this remark to scare Freddy. But she was looking at the snapshots on his desk, and talking about Sheriff Deputy Dog, as she sometimes sarcastically referred to Freddy.

"Not bad for forty-something. Looks like he might be a jerk sometimes. But there's hope in his eyes."

Cindy smiled and sashayed across the room—if such a thing was possible in her oversized black gun belt and baggy uniform. She took a seat before the dispatch radio, surrounded by a pile of paperwork. The Garrison uniform did not look like a bag on Officer Betts.

After the Public Works Building was built as a medical center, it became an automotive garage for a while. The tiny jail cell—which was used to house the occasional drunk—was once used for tire storage. Only once, when the local gynecologist got hammered and struck a tree on the way home from a New Year's party, did the building ever hold a person of the caliber for which it had been built. By the time he made bail, the drunken physician smelled like Dr. Goodwrench.

There were public citations and framed clippings on the walls, most of them about concerned citizens who had performed heroic feats in a foreign land—New York City. Freddy looked up from his desk to see a green-eyed detective with graying tufts at his ears staring at him through his window.

Moe Tilden snapped a butt in the gutter and walked into the corner deli, advertising Lotto, keys, coffee, and "many other items." The place had all the class and permanent character of broken white stucco.

The phone in Freddy's station office sounded and Cindy fell to the floor trying to get to it, knocking over a pile of tickets she had been studying. Police work was hazardous in Garrison.

"Shit," Cindy said. She knocked over her radio, which went into alarm mode: *Dweep. Dweep. Dweep.*

Freddy sighed and looked across the street. A beautiful brown-haired woman was strapping a child into a seat. He smiled with recognition and faint desire. Freddy saw the little girl, holding a plush turtle. The woman put the stuffed green animal on the top of her van as she strapped the child in.

Dweep. Dweep. Dweep.

"Dispatch," Cindy announced. "Can you hold a second?"

Freddy watched as a car—a blue Olds he now recognized as belonging to Ray Donlan—pulled into the lot. The beautiful woman smiled at the cop. They were all from the same town and tribe. Donlan, Rucker, and Lagonda walked into the deli as the woman drove the van away. Freddy watched as the forgotten green turtle fell into a puddle. He lurched out of his seat, diving toward the muddy bubbles again.

NINE

The cops were standing at the window, drinking coffee. They had been up all night, and although haggard, were still sharp. They were even excited. They stared out into the street, each of them silently remembering a piece of the previous nights. They were dressed in the kind of cotton casual shirts and loose slacks that screamed "off duty." Still, though, Donlan wore brown tasseled loafers. But the other guys wore sneakers that falsified their own athletic ability. Once Rucker had worked the New York marathon along Fourth Avenue in Sunset Park, Brooklyn. That was as close as he'd ever come to exercise. He had been known to beat suspects who made him run after them.

Their minds were working now. They had pulled the great caper. Lagonda, like the worst of the crackheads he had ever arrested or beaten, talked too much.

"You were perfect last night, Ray," he whispered. "It was perfect."

Donlan stared out into the street. So did Rucker. Tilden walked in behind them and went to order a coffee.

The cops did not recognize the green-eyed man as anything but a stranger to their town.

"Hey, Ray," Tilden said, walking, with his container of black coffee, to the counter where they stored the milk and sugar.

"Hey, Moe," Donlan said. He was not surprised to see Internal Affairs on the case, just jarred slightly to see Tilden here so fast. The lieutenant swallowed his surprise as the other cops looked silently to him for their lead.

"I'm sorry about your nephew," Tilden said. He removed the lid from his coffee.

"Yeah. He was a good kid," Donlan said, gesturing to the others. "We were up all night with it."

Tilden took a step toward Donlan, who was opening the milk canisters and dumping them into his coffee. The lieutenant measured the other cops as he emptied the precise amount of milk into his cup.

"Uh," Donlan continued, "I know you need to talk to me. I'll come in next week sometime, how's that? Rucker here is coming in early for you—tomorrow."

Tilden was in his role now, just one of the four cops in the room playing their parts. Tilden offered his hand to Rucker.

"Hey," he said. "How you doing? Moe Tilden."

Rucker looked as though he might cut Moe's hand off. He replied, warily, "Yeah. Hey."

Lagonda offered a limp hand. Tilden went back to his coffee. He stirred the sugar into it. (Donlan was saccharin at best.)

"Moe here was my classmate—at the academy—back in the day," Donlan said. He was playing for the other cops. "Before he fell in love with this redhead at IA and transferred."

Tilden smiled and kept stirring in his sugar.

"Is that the way it went, Ray?"

Tilden was not asking a question, just showing Donlan that he was not to be trifled with.

"So," Donlan said. "What brings you to our fair city?"

Tilden blinked and looked out the window. "Heard it

was a way of life over here," Tilden said. "I wanted to see it firsthand."

Donlan offered a challenging smirk and raised his hands in mock protest. "What are we—like, the Amish now?"

It was a good line but the other two gave it more attention than it deserved. Tilden smiled, licked the red stirrer, and put the cover on his coffee. They were done, for now.

"When does that Arby's open up?" he asked.

"Couple of months."

Tilden moved to the door. "Gonna take a chunk out of this place."

"I'll still be here," Ray Donlan said.

Tilden nodded and exited, saying, "I know you will."

The cops followed him to the window and began to curse. Donlan's face grimaced with murderous intent.

"The fucking rat."

"They ain't real cops," Lagonda said. "They ain't really ever done nothing. They don't know nothing. If this is what we got to worry about, we got nothing to worry about." He was that obtuse.

They watched Tilden walk to his car and pull a piece of paper from his windshield. From a distance, it looked like a parking ticket. The lieutenant examined it closely. It was a promotion for a July Fourth celebration sponsored by the Garrison Volunteer Fire Department. In the city this event would be a brawl. The investigator folded the sheet and put it in his pocket.

In Garrison, he realized, it was all one party, one big softball team with guns. He smiled and looked up. Sheriff Freddy Heflin was walking down the street with a crushed, muddy green turtle in his hands. He did not even see Tilden.

"Thought you gave me a ticket," the stranger told the sheriff.

"Hmm?" Freddy replied.

"You the sheriff?"

Freddy was not paying enough attention to be insulted. He studied the man in the brown tweed jacket briefly. He didn't even recognize him as the green-eyed man staring in his window minutes before.

"Oh, yeah," Freddy said.

Then a bottle broke in the alley and kids began to scream. Freddy switched into his town sheriff mode.

"Just a second," Freddy told the best investigator in the modern history of the NYPD's Internal Affairs unit. "Gordon, get out of there!"

A grungy kid holding another kid by the neck, and a couple of others, quit the fight and ran.

"Go on," Freddy said. The sheriff turned back to Tilden and touched his bangaged nose. He stuck the turtle under his arm, unsure who this man was, but embarrassed.

"How long you been sheriff?" Moe Tilden asked.

"Hmm," Freddy replied. "Oh. Ten years."

"That's great," Tilden said. He had already decided by then that the sheriff was probably not going to be even mentally capable of helping him. Consciously, anyway.

"Lotta cops here, huh?" Tilden continued.

"Yeah."

"Well, it's a great gig," Tilden said as he pulled out his card. "I'm sure you're busy, but keep my card. I'm with a special unit—in the city. In case . . . you know . . . you want to talk."

Freddy read the operative words: MAURICE TILDEN. NYPD. INTERNAL AFFAIRS. He got the idea. But by the time he looked up, Tilden was in his car and gone. That was the way the great investigators were. You never saw them coming, or going.

TEN

Freddy drove through the track housing that was the heart of Garrison. The homes were colonials and swollen ranches for the most part, or split-level variations on a theme that had been invented by the father of the suburban life, William Levitt. He built Levittown, Long Island, and America had followed his lead into the cul-de-sac of housing fame, or infamy. It all depended on how you felt about the green, watered, suburban life. You were safe from crime, certainly, but protected perhaps too tightly from life's seasoning and strange episodes.

New York City cops escaped all that temperature and indulgence when they came home. Their wives could be raging fevers of a different sort. It was deadly boring to be so disconnected from the city and its excitement once you had experienced it. Marriages were ruined by alcohol and memory. Drinking took cops to some other place. Memory kept some of their wives from ever returning to that place. The worst of the cops' marriages saw the young officer coming home to a prisoner. Garrison, indeed.

Freddy drove the road that bisected the split-level houses and listened to the all-news radio station in the idle of the afternoon. He drove as he rebandaged his nose. The stuffed turtle, now filthy and mangled, was on the seat beside him. The radio throbbed with the news: "And this

59

morning's top story: A white hero cop jumps off the GWB after shooting two black teenagers. The dead teenagers were reportedly unarmed."

There were basketball nets hanging from every garage. In New Jersey, one of the greatest legends in the history of Madison Square Garden and Knicks basketball became a United States senator. But in the Long Island town where one of his greatest teammates lived, the predominantly white homeowners had passed a local ordinance restricting where and when you could hang a hoop. The papers all decided it was a race thing. Black families, the worst bigots believed, wouldn't move into a home where they couldn't hang a basketball net. The NYPD cops didn't believe in surrender. Their kids played basketball and dreamed of playing it at Princeton, a great white basketball school.

As he drove, Freddy passed one home without a basketball rim. The name on the mailbox read TUNNEY. For a while there, the home of the lynched police officer had become a national shrine. People still placed flower baskets on the lawn. But once Glenn Tunney's lawn had been covered with hundreds of roses and blue NYPD funeral arrangements. Occasionally, in the dark of night, a drunken bagpiper from the Emerald Society would wander by and play taps on Glenn Tunney's front lawn. No one in the town ever complained.

Freddy drove on until he reached a mailbox that read RANDONE. As he approached the door, a Doberman on a chain barked. Freddy knocked, and then knocked again. The Doberman was thrilled to be working. Freddy could hear voices, but he turned, and started to walk away.

"Jesus. I'm sorry," a woman shouted over his shoulder. The door swung open and revealed the beautiful brown-haired woman from the parking lot. Liz Randone was wearing a flowered, open blouse. Her hair was up and she had a hand on her hip. Her lips and teeth were beauty-pageant perfect. They weren't even capped. She wore a gold crucifix on a chain around her neck. She was a dream, Freddy Heflin's fantasy girl, still. He could hear a baby crying in the background.

"That's okay," Freddy said, smiling bashfully. "I was gonna have the base call you . . ."

Liz studied the cop and then saw the turtle.

"Oh, Freddy," she cooed. "Look what you found."

She took the crushed animal and hugged it.

"She is gonna be so happy. Her daddy won it at the fair last year. I left it on the van . . ."

"Yeah. I know. From my window, I saw."

Liz liked the idea of Freddy still watching her. She smiled wider, infected by Freddy's dopey grin. But just as suddenly, her smile disappeared. "That's awful about Ray's nephew, huh?" she said.

The baby began to cry, loudly. She had just discovered she was alone, and that scared her.

"Hey, Caroline! Come on, now. Daddy is trying to sleep."

At this hour of the day, only two types of men dozed in well-kept suburban homes, the joke went, cops and robbers. Joey Randone was a New York City cop working steady midnights. This was the greatest cop gig in the world—a suburban life and no rush hour. But the hours made for cheaters and a shitty marriage. The Randones had all of that. Every day. Freddy thought about this and stared at the studded cross on her neck, remembering. He broke off his stare and the watery memory.

"I heard they're gonna do the service here," she said. Freddy nodded and she touched his bandaged nose.

"Ouch, what happened to you?"

"Little accident. Chasing a speeder."

The child was yelling louder. "Mommy, come see. Mommy, come see."

"Just a second," she said. She liked the company of the easy sheriff. Liz crossed into the room with the turtle, and exclaimed, "Baby, look what the sheriff found." She brushed it off and handed it to the baby, who calmed at seeing her old friend.

"Freddy, you want some coffee?"

"No, I'm fine."

He stepped timidly into the foyer. He studied the pictures on the wall: a child's drawing, a photograph of Joey Randone in uniform, a portrait of Liz at sixteen, a beauty crown on her head. He knew that picture well. Liz was a forbidden place, though Freddy wanted to be there. The photograph of Joey Randone stared coldly at Freddy.

"So," Liz said, "I hope you caught him."

"Hmm? Caught who, Liz?"

"The speeder."

"Oh. Yeah."

"You know," Liz continued then, "I was thinking of calling you. I mean, not you, but one of your deputies."

"Why? What's up?"

"Oh, someone's been dumping garbage. Garbage bags." She pointed toward the four garbage bags by the road. Three white bags and a black one. Freddy eagerly pulled out his black leather investigator's pad and a pen.

"Uh-huh. Is that them?"

"There's just one. The rest are mine."

"Okay, Liz. They put the one bag in with yours."

She was kind of angry to be put off so easily.

"This isn't the first time. They have been pulling this shit for weeks, slipping it in. Why? One bag isn't good enough for an investigation?"

Freddy erased a number in his book. He was that quick

and diligent. "One bag is enough. Yeah. A beer bottle is enough as far as I'm concerned."

"Damn right. Besides, I use white bags. Theirs are black. Some cheap shit. The bags are *garbage*."

She did not mean to be funny. Freddy scribbled more furiously in his pad.

"I didn't tell Joey—'cause he thinks he's gotta take care of policing the house, too. Not that he doesn't think much of local—you guys—but I know he would probably shoot somebody—"

"I'll take care of it," Freddy said. "He's got the city to worry about, right?"

Liz nodded and Freddy smiled. She was enchanting, and he hoped his own eyes were sparkling.

Freddy walked to the end of the Randone driveway and pushed a pencil through the black garbage bag. Liz watched him from the window for a moment, then moved away.

Freddy flipped through paper plates, bottles of beer, corn on the cob and, finally, a stained envelope.

Ray Donlan
31 Dallas Drive

Freddy drove to the house right away. He stood at the door of the split-level and rang the bell, the soiled evidence in his hand. Before him stood a busty middle-aged blonde. She had a snarl on her lips and a cigarette in her mouth. In her day, which was ten years gone by, Rose could break up a dozen marriages just by poking her blond head in a Queens precinct. But those days were a memory. Now she mostly broke liquor bottles. She was Garrison's most well-known suburban, and perhaps even lethal, weapon. She had been outlawed from the Four Aces Tavern years ago.

"What if I said I didn't know where the bag came from," Rose snarled.

"I'd take your word for it, Rose. Is, ah, Ray home?"

"Taking care of our little visitor," Rose said without explanation. Freddy didn't need any. He played with the phone bill. Rose stared at the envelope. She was like the most transparent of criminals, the ones who wanted to get caught.

"I get my garbage picked up every Tuesday."

"All right. Thanks for your time."

Freddy began to walk back to his patrol car.

But Rose wasn't finished. "You tell Joey to come to me himself and talk about it if he thinks I got no right."

Freddy stopped dead, then turned around. "Rose, I want to believe you when you tell me something."

"Oh you do, do you?"

"Did you dump those bags or not?"

Rose almost growled. For a moment Freddy thought the lipstick would melt off her upper lip.

"This is not a law and order problem, genius. If you catch my drift. You tell Joey Randone that if he doesn't like my garbage he should stop soiling my sheets."

Rose was miraculously nonchalent—even daring Freddy to proceed with the investigation. She might have snapped his spine with her reckless glare.

"Rose, you can't just dump garbage on other people's property."

"But that glamour boy—he can throw away a woman just like she was garbage when he's done with her, and that's okay? Is that what you're saying, Sheriff?"

He wasn't saying a word. They stared at each other as a phone rang in the background.

"Are you going to tell Ray about this?" Rose asked.

Freddy shook his head. She dragged hard on her ciga-

rette, disappointed by the sheriff's answer. The phone rang
again and she left him there as she spun and slammed the
door.

As Freddy started to back his squad car out of the Donlan driveway, the blue Olds Delta 88 pulled in beside him.
Ray, the only occupant of the car, jumped out. He was surprised to see Freddy in his driveway.

"What's up, Freddy? Decided to give me that ticket?"

Freddy put his car in park but did not shut off the engine. He was not staying on this investigation any longer.

"No, Ray. Someone has just been dumping garbage."

Freddy wanted to give Ray room to fall. All most people
needed to fall was arrogance and confidence. Freddy was
playing the country bumpkin, and it didn't take a whole lot
of acting. He *was* a bumpkin. But he now knew that Ray's
wife, was, or at least had been, humping Liz Randone's husband. Ray bit Freddy's bait, hard.

"Oh, a *fel-ony*," Ray said, meaning the garbage. Freddy
smiled. There was no law against wife-dumping or garbage-
swapping among the blue acquaintances of Garrison, New
Jersey. Freddy Heflin waved good-bye and drove off to find
a pinball machine.

There were flashing lights up ahead. Deputy Bill Geisler
stood beside his car. He had pulled over a rusted maroon
Chevy Impala, a black man and woman inside the car.
Above them the Garrison water tower rose against the orange sky. Manhattan was just starting to brighten across
the river. The bridge seemed to grow out of the marshlands.

"They were a few over," Geisler said. "I'm running a
plate check."

Freddy nodded, turned, and looked down to the water.
As he stared at the foul graffiti-scarred overpasses, a concerto filled his one good ear and he was back under the same

interstate waterway again. It was the 1970s and Freddy saw himself eating a bag lunch under the overpass. He was nineteen years old again. He saw the construction machines and heard the loud curses as the car hurtled past. It came off the bridge and down into the water. It came down nose first, green and loud into the water. He didn't see anyone in the car, then or now.

He stood, silent and awestruck. He did not think. It was different from all the football games, and the gaping holes in the defensive line. He just saw, understood, and reacted as the car sank in a flurry of bubbles. In the next moment, he dove. He felt the bubbles against his skin as he dove deeper and deeper. He saw her face against the window. It was clear, perfect and young. But her eyes were closed. Freddy pulled open the door and pulled the girl to shore. She wasn't breathing. He began to breathe into her mouth, until she finally opened her eyes.

She was the beauty queen from Garrison High School. Her name was Liz; Freddy knew that much even before he pulled her from the water and breathed life into her. Only weeks later, following a raging infection, did the ringing disappear from his ears. The damage grew as the girl ignored him. And as Freddy became more deaf in one ear, Liz became more blinded to his feeling for her. They circled each other like orbiting celestial bodies, but never kissed again after that moment when Freddy passed oxygen and being into Liz's limp body.

The headlines from the papers still hung in his home. His own wife never bothered to throw them out. "Local Boy Saves Drowning Teen. Hero in hospital with ear infection from icy waters."

The photo showed young Freddy standing by the water. He had a bandage over his ear. Liz, the beauty queen, smiled down on him from her high school portrait.

He liked having the newspaper clipping around. It reminded him that once, when it counted, he had mattered. He had shown unconditional courage, and it had cost him an ear. He would do it all again, or so he imagined.

The angry voices brought him back to the police car stop. The rusted Impala was rolling past Freddy. The driver was waving a ticket menacingly.

"We come here to watch the sunset," the woman shrieked. "And you pull this."

"Speeding, my ass," said the driver. "Fucking racist pigs."

Freddy did not argue, although he wished as they passed him, that the deafness had spread to his other ear. He checked the rearview mirror for Geisler.

"All done," the deputy said. And Freddy was not ashamed.

Freddy was sitting at his desk talking on the phone a few minutes later.

"Liz—all I'm saying is that I think it's going to stop."

Liz actually hissed into his good ear.

"It was Joey's little bitch, wasn't it? Sending messages."

Cindy Betts heard his voice and peered into Freddy's office, checking. She didn't miss much of anything.

"Uh," Freddy said. "Can you hold a second?"

He punched the Hold button. Cindy crossed to Freddy and sat beside him. She looked very comfortable.

"I'm on the phone."

"I can see that."

"How about I meet you across the street in fifteen minutes."

Cindy made a face. This did not sound like police work.

And if it wasn't, Cindy was hoping to be the sheriff's extra-curricular activity.

"Look, I'm sorry. How about tomorrow? I'll take you someplace nice. Okay?"

Cindy let this hang in the air. You didn't have to be a cop to hear the deception in Freddy's voice. She walked out, slamming the door. Freddy hit the Hold button.

"Liz, Liz?"

"What?"

"Do you want me to talk to Joey?"

Freddy glanced at the old newspaper story about them. Twenty years later, he still couldn't hear and she still couldn't see.

"Talk to him? Freddy? Why? You didn't marry him."

"No, Liz. But I am your friend."

"I gotta go, Freddy."

And then Liz was gone, again.

ELEVEN

Freddy Heflin was *home* again, fat with a roll of quarters in his pocket. The sheriff was sipping a drink at the bar in the Four Aces Tavern, doing crosswords. Most nights the place was the same, not unlike a police precinct. Sometimes the names on the walls changed, a new hero would be added, but a cop bar is as constant as a cop locker room. Tonight it was crowded with about twenty off-duty cops. Most of them wore at least one piece of clothing that read "NYPD." It was all the badge they needed in Garrison.

Frank Lagonda was entertaining some rookies by the vending machines. "No, I am telling you," Lagonda said. "This EMS motherfucker—he thinks he's Zorro—he takes the gun in his hand. *State's evidence.* And he's waving it."

The rookies were electric with this pathetic version of the story. Lagonda had only recently started working the street. He had been a union delegate for years in a Queens precinct, the 103rd in South Jamaica. During the worst of the crack madness, a uniformed rookie patrolman had been executed while sitting in a marked patrol car outside a drug witness's house. It became national news. The dealers said they were giving a message to the cops. Their boss had just been imprisoned for life: We lose one, you lose one. George Bush had campaigned for president wearing the kid's badge. To hear Lagonda talk about this hero cop in the Four

Aces was to think he had been in the patrol car with the rookie. But Lagonda was all narrative and no action. He wore medals on his tunic for years of service, not valor. He was in police work for the pension and the wickedness of the badge.

"I was gonna shoot the fucking medic myself," Lagonda said.

"You should have," one of the kids said.

"They can have a felony record and get a job on an ambulance," Lagonda said. "And if they beat you to a crime scene, *they* rob the body. They *is* the perps."

"Right," one of the kids said.

"A couple of months ago, I saw this Asian medic working a double homicide in the Bronx," Lagonda continued. "I am looking at this bitch and I realize, holy shit, I arrested this bitch a dozen times for prostitution, myself. How can she have gotten this job? Who investigates these people?"

"I read about this," said one rookie.

"Right," Lagonda continued. "After I screamed, the Department of Investigation finished their background check. She had two hundred fucking prostitution arrests. The last one was sixteen years ago. But I don't care if she became Mother Fucking Teresa. No pross can be working alongside me."

"She could give AIDS to the patients," one cop said. "Bleed on *them* and kill them."

The laugh was huge. Lagonda was bullshitting, of course. He only recognized the woman in the newspaper, after the story broke, as a prostitute he had frequented when he lived south of Garrison fifteen years ago. He remembered her as the last stop before the Lincoln Tunnel.

"Fucking perps," Lagonda said. "The city is allowing perps to work our cases and motherfuckers to hang us in jail cells."

Leo Crasky stood near the men's room door, smoking. He was a respected snoop, one of the stalwarts in the detectives' union. He was a legitimate tough guy, a wiry fellow who could outsmart any thug he couldn't outpunch. He lived by a curious motto: Good guys can scheme, too.

"No, no, you're using the short form," Crasky said. "For us, for cops, there are tons of deductions. I write off newspapers and magazines because a detective has to know what's going on in the world."

"How about Yankee tickets?" one rookie asked.

"Hey, you gotta follow the bad guys wherever they go," Crasky said.

"I heard you could refuse to pay anything and just say you ain't a citizen of the United States," another kid said.

"What are you?" Crasky bellowed. "Some kind of communist?"

They roared.

Crasky was a legend in the Bronx, where he had worked for years in the 46th precinct before he quit drinking so much and reclaimed his mind. Now he worked in Manhattan North Homicide. Everyone loved him there as a father figure. He was a dying breed, a dinosaur who had worked the street for twenty years and rarely left the precinct. A beer drinker without peer, back then Leo Crasky served as the precinct gas station attendant, cell attendant, and assistant station house officer. They had a name for this duty. Leo Crasky was the precinct "broom."

Over the years he had established himself in a series of astonishing events. One day he was given the job of filling in for the commander's regular driver. He walked out into the parking lot, started the boss's car, and stepped on the gas pedal instead of the brake. Crasky smashed into a pole and careened through a set of metal doors into the precinct vestibule. He was said to have calmly shut off the car, walked into the captain's office, and plunked himself down.

"Boss," Crasky said. "I just got into a car accident and I want you know I didn't even start drinking yet."

Young cops had been particularly fond of blackening out the numbers on his combination lock. As he'd squinted to read them, they had yelled, "Why don't you go home, you old fart, and get some glasses?" They stopped the torture after Crasky pulled his gun and shot off his lock and several others. On another occasion he took exception to the loudness of a boom box. In the precinct locker room, Leo asked the kid, nicely, to turn the noise down. When he refused, Crasky pulled his gun and executed the stereo with a single shot, yelling, "I'll show you. Take that."

He was always either drinking or cooping—sleeping on the job, perhaps in a car parked in the lot. He was also supposed to watch prisoners in the holding cell. One night, they recalled, Crasky fell asleep, and a kid hung himself. They discovered the prisoner and brought him back to life.

"Don't worry, the kid is going to make it," the cops told him.

Crasky went from weak to furious in a second. He strode over to the suicidal victim after he regained consciousness, and kicked him in the head.

"I will kill you," he screamed. "Nobody dies on my watch."

So, everyone loved Leo Crasky. He was the real deal, they said. Especially since he'd cut back on his drinking. As Crasky gave tax advice, Figs emerged from the men's room, wiping his nose. Like Freddy, Figs was alone. But unlike Freddy, who was alone with his deafness, Figs was alone with his demons. He was a dark man, given to unexplainable rage and gigantic mood swings. Ordinarily, he did not need drugs to be whacked. Once, when he was on a precinct fishing trip, one of the guys he was with had pulled a fluke out of the water. Figs pulled his gun out and started to shoot at the fish. And laugh. The cop dropped the pole and jumped in the water.

"Are you crazy?" the cop later asked Figs.

"I hope so," Figs replied.

The cops didn't trust Figs they way they trusted Lagonda, Crasky, and Jack Rucker, the bar's resident psychopath. Figs thought there were bigger things than being a cop. And that was dangerous. Rucker watched him walk to the bar and sit beside Freddy. Rucker liked to call Freddy "Sheriff Square Badge" and "Johnny Rent-A-Cop" when Freddy wasn't listening. As Freddy Heflin couldn't hear squat, Rucker offered the slights all the time.

"I knew this guy who wanted off the job so bad, he wanted his partner to shoot him in the leg," a thin cop told Rucker.

Rucker laughed and replied, "I shot one of my first partners and didn't really mean it."

The thin cop dropped his dart, and Rucker laughed louder.

"I didn't mean to hit him with the first couple of rounds, anyway."

Jack Rucker was a sick bastard. He prided himself on mental illness.

Figs sipped his drink and winked at Freddy. The sheriff was intoxicated with all the conversation and enjoying the drunk. The was *alive* with the tales of other cops. Besides, the kids were hogging his pinball machine. Delores, the barmaid, refilled their drinks.

"How they gonna bury him?" she wanted to know. "With no body?"

"Ray Donlan will bury his baseball card collection if he

has to," Figs said. "You don't want to delay the ceremony. You lose the media attention. You lose the platform."

"They know who the kids were?" a cop asked.

"Bebos," Figs said. "From Newark."

"Who's Bebos?" Delores asked.

"It's not a guy, Del," Figs said and chuckled.

Freddy interrupted. "Bebos are a drug gang, Del. Jamaicans. It's short for 'Who you be, bro?' "

Impressed, Figs winked at Freddy. Freddy smiled. It was white, racist white cop *bullshit*. But Freddy repeated the bullshit in the correct NYPD manner.

The entire bar fell silent as the eleven o'clock news came on. Someone even turned down the jukebox and purposely tilted the pinball machine. The hard-edged television reporter was known to trade anyone above the rank of sergeant a hum job in the back of her TV van for a scoop. Now she was comforting a crying woman, the mother of one of the kids shot on the bridge: "Cyril Johns met with the mother of one of the slain teens, calling for a human blockage of the bridge tomorrow."

The bar became completely silent as Cyril Johns spoke directly into the camera: "A drunk white cop jumps off a bridge, that doesn't erase the murder of two black children."

Two cops in the back hissed. One yelled, "Black cunt." A third bounced a Budweiser can off the television. A fourth muttered, "And these people wonder why Mark Fuhrman exists?"

On the television the reporter said that the mayor, while attending the Giants-Jets preseason game up the road, had responded to reports that the cops had planted evidence on the bridge.

"Yes, we are looking into that," the mayor said. "There may have been some . . . irregularities . . . that we are looking into."

There was booing. The jukebox came on even before the station went to the weather. The conversations, much angrier now, resumed.

"The Diagonal Rule," Figs said.

"The what?" Freddy asked.

As they spoke, Joey Randone, about thirty-five, a strikingly handsome man who was almost angrily lean, entered the bar. The cops yelled to him.

"The Diagonal Rule," Figs said. "Red light. Don't fight. Make a right. More important than the Golden Rule. If Superboy knew that, he'd be alive."

Figs smiled at Joey Randone, who walked toward him but ignored him. He stuck his fist into a bowl of pretzels next to Freddy. Randone was a tough fellow. He wore a gray New York Giants T-shirt cut off at the shoulders, and a miniature gold copy of his police badge around his neck. The NYPD was his cross, his savior.

"Freddy, heard you saved Ollie the turtle today."

Freddy was playing with a red plastic stirrer. But he looked up, and smiled.

"Uh . . . yeah."

"What happened to your face, Freddy?"

Freddy touched the bandage on his nose again.

"Listen, Joey, there is something we should probably talk about."

Joey grabbed some pretzels.

"What's that, Freddy?"

Figs did not like being ignored. He spoke in a taunting, even singsong voice.

"Pretty boy Joe-Joe bet against the Bulls, what are you, some kind of high roller?"

"Fuck you, Figs. I had twelve points."

The championship game had been played last month. But the wound was still fresh. Figs would not desist. Like

Dennis Rodman, Figs wanted an audience. He spoke even louder.

"Against the Bulls? Twelve points was twelve reasons for you to become a child. To revert to some prepubescent state. You should have prayed before bedtime for those pussies."

"I don't have to pray for anything," Randone said. "I had *twelve fucking points.*"

Freddy disappeared into the pretzel bowl.

"Against the four-time NBA champs," Figs continued. "You night boys watch too much *Oprah* and too many O.J. reruns when you should be catching some z's."

"At least I'm not putting my paycheck up my nose." There was laughter from behind them. "I ain't the one pissing my money away," Joey said, then walked off waving his middle finger in the air.

"That was your inner child making that bet, Joey. Little Joey with a '69 Mets poster taped above his bed."

At a back table, Joey grabbed his crotch.

"Figsy, why don't you unzip me and bite my prepubescent state. You bite it thick and hard."

There were oohs and cackles in the back.

"Fuck you, Joey. Thick is a word best used to describe your brain."

Figs turned and spoke in a low voice to Freddy.

"Goddamned child. Kid with a badge."

"Huh," Freddy said. He was playing thick to the whole conversation.

"With a badge," Figs said loudly. "That's how shitheads argue. They point to their cock. A dumb fuck like that in our PD—how does that make you feel? With his connections, that is a detective you are looking at. He'll have the gold shield in four or five years. He's riding the fast track. Fuck his big dick talk. He's got a real rocket in his pocket."

"I don't give a shit," Freddy said.

"Yeah. You like eating doughnuts?"

Freddy could only shrug and smirk.

"I say it's okay to be jealous. It's very—you know, primeval—I mean, a primitive condition. You save a chick's life. And from it—from risking yourself and saving her sorry ass—you go deaf. As a result . . ."

"In one ear . . ."

". . . you can't become a cop."

Figs shook his head. He needed to use the bathroom and talk to the guys in the back. Freddy lit a cigarette and started to watch a television drama about New York City cops. From the back of the room, Freddy heard some loud voice. Donlan was there and Freddy hadn't even seen him come into the tavern.

"Bullshit," Figs said. "What is this *omerta?*"

"Sit down, Gary," Donlan said.

"Hey," Figs continued. "If IA is going to hang me by the balls, it ain't gonna be over missing evidence."

"Six grams of coke missing," Lagonda said. "That ain't no white-socks violation."

"You bought that big old house," Rucker said, sneering and accusatory. "Maybe you are looking to get out from under."

"Hey, down, boy," Donlan said.

"You're damn right I am. What is up your ass, Jack? You getting by without gravy? FUCK. I was putting out Ray's fires when you were sucking your mama's tittie."

"Sit down," Donlan said.

"Or even better," Rucker suggested, "get the fuck out—"

"Fuck you. You fucking child."

"At least I'm not shacking up with a PR whore," Rucker said.

Some cops even laughed. Figs stood his ground.

"You're supposed to fuck 'em, Gary," Rucker continued. "Not open a methadone clinic."

Rucker snickered and looked for support from the room. It was silent. He had gone too far.

"What?" Rucker said. "It's true."

Suddenly, Figs was across the table. He pummeled Rucker and they grabbed each other. It was a hockey fight, mostly, all pulling and missed overhand rights. The chairs fell backward.

Freddy rose from his stool.

His face bloodied, Rucker suddenly drew his revolver, waving it wildly. As this was action and not make-believe, Lagonda stepped back. Donlan, still seated, waved his hand.

"Oh, for Christ's sake," he said.

But Rucker did not move his gun and Figs did not move his chest. He grabbed Rucker by the head and shoved it into the dartboard. Figs was not a make-believe tough guy. He grabbed a dart and held it inside the cop's nose. Freddy had seen a scene like this with Jack Nicholson as Roman Polanski's victim in the movie *Chinatown*.

"Hey, hey," the plodding sheriff said. He was ignored.

"Oww," Rucker screeched. "Jesus Christ."

"You got a problem with me helping a girl in trouble?" Figs said, the steel dart point in Rucker's nose. "You have a problem with that?"

"No. NO!" Rucker said. "You're a fucking humanitarian."

Rucker lowered his gun, and yelped against the pain from the dart. Figs walked him across the room.

"You think you are so bad, little boy."

Figs pressed Rucker's face against the portrait of a young blue-eyed cop on the wall. The nameplate on the cop read OFFICER GLENN TUNNEY.

"You see that?" Figs shouted, madly. "That was my part-ner. *That was a cop.*"

Ray Donlan, the controlled man, was the only person still seated in the bar. He slowly rose.

"*Enough.* Let go of him, Figs."

Crasky moved to take the gun from Rucker's hand. Figs removed the dart and Rucker fell to the floor. Donlan glared at Figs.

"Go home," the lieutenant said.

Figs looked up, bleeding from the lip, and measured Donlan.

"Freddy, get him out of here," Ray said.

"Come on Figs . . ."

Figs shook Freddy off with a shoulder spin and refo-cused on Ray Donlan.

"Ray, don't shut me out. Okay? Yes, you are still the big man. You found us a sweet town. Got us low-interest loans. Financed the residency requirements. Hey, I was grateful. I am grateful. But don't forget two years ago. Who you came to when you needed your own ass covered."

Donlan was smoldering. Lagonda, feeling suddenly brave, made a move to stand up. Donlan held him with a wave of the hand.

Figs turned, and pointing at the portrait of Glenn Tun-ney, said, "It's not my fault you can't look at him, Ray. You sit in that chair. With your back to him. You want it to go away. But I'm still here, Ray. In for a penny, in for a pound. Just don't shut me out."

Figs walked to the coatrack and pulled on his nylon NYPD jacket. Freddy followed him to the door. Everyone watched, frozen. They waited until Figs, taking his time, rolled up his sleeves and exited. At the last step, Figs spun around and faced Freddy, smiling.

"You should have hit me, Freddy. Ray woulda liked that."

TWELVE

They stayed too late in the Four Aces that night. There was no leaving after the departure of Figs. Later, as Donlan looked to the door, he made eye contact with Joey Randone, talking to another cop. Randone broke off the eye contact. To Donlan, that was an admission. Not that he needed one.

"Later," Donlan said and waved. And meant it.

Rucker studied Freddy as he walked back to their table with a beer. "Someone's dropping a dime," Rucker said. The cop checked Freddy with a look. "We just can't keep *it* here for two weeks, waiting."

Freddy sat beside Donlan and the controlled man looked at the sheriff tensely. Donlan winced as Rucker continued.

"I mean, Freddy's new girl pulls us over, Tilden showed up here with that grin. We got some *loose* ends."

"Cindy is cool," Freddy said. "She didn't see nothing."

Donlan was clearly uncomfortable talking about this with Freddy.

"I'm sorry," Freddy said. And stood.

"Sit down, Freddy."

"That's okay. I don't want to interrupt."

"Sit down, Freddy."

Freddy sat with the conspirators. Like a new kid in school sitting with the guys for the first time at the coolest lunch table, Freddy talked and smiled too much. He was with *them*. And the sheriff was giddy with the attention, and the beer, and the involvement.

"Freddy," Donlan said, "you know that polyp they took out of my ass?"

Freddy nodded, uneasy, unsure where this was going.

"Well, sometimes, when I look at Jackie Rucker, here . . ."

Rucker actually grinned. He had no sense of his limitations.

"The cop who did such a masterful job on the bridge last night—sometimes—I think—someone planted that polyp, watered it, gave it a badge—and now that piece of my ass is sitting here grinning at me like a fucking hyena."

Rucker lost his smile as Donlan decided how to proceed. Freddy peeled the label off his beer.

"You know that I'm a man, Ray," Rucker tried.

"Freddy is my man. Unfortunately, he's on the wrong side of the river."

"It don't mean you can't trust me," Freddy said. *"With anything."*

"I do trust you, Freddy," Ray said. "I trust you to keep the kids from killing themselves on prom night. I trust you to suggest a good opera record for my sister at Christmas."

Freddy had the sense to be insulted. He was disappointed.

"I'm serious, Ray."

"Freddy," Ray said, looking up. "Every day when I'm away, I trust you with my town. Maybe I don't trust you with 'anything,' but I trust you with my home and my family. And to me that's everything."

Donlan pointed the dart at Freddy. Freddy squirmed, but not as much as Randone, who walked out the door. Donlan rose and walked to the dartboard. He buried the dart in the cork until it squeaked in protest.

* * *

Later, as Freddy left the bar, sighing with the weight of the day's events, a Garrison patrol car pulled up. Bill Geisler jumped out.

"We got—uh—a domestic," he announced.

THIRTEEN

The Doberman on the chain began to bark again as soon as he saw Freddy's car. The Randone house was more intimidating at night. Joey Randone, in boxer shorts, was pounding at the front door.

"Come on, baby. Fuck."

"Fuck you," Liz shot back from the other side of the door.

Finally, Freddy and Bill started to get out of the car. Randone whirled on them as dozens of similarly crazed husbands and boyfriends had whenever they'd arrived to investigate a domestic dispute on their beat.

"Go home, Freddy. Everything is hunky-dory."

"You mind if we check up on Liz?" Freddy asked. Joey had two new cuts on his neck.

"Yes, I mind." He sat down.

Freddy knocked on the door. His deputy kneeled to check Randone's neck.

"This is nasty," Bill said of the glass cut. "Let me get the kit."

Freddy knocked again.

"Fuck you."

"Liz? It's Freddy."

Joey looked up, sullen.

"Does Ray know?" he asked the sheriff. Freddy didn't answer.

"She hit me with a Listerine bottle."

"I thought they were made with plastic now," the deputy tried, returning with the ointment and bandages.

Freddy knocked again.

"She ain't opening the door," Joey said.

"Goddammit," Liz said, cracking the door. And then, "Hey, Freddy."

"*You* okay?"

She nodded. But her eyes were red. Joey saw her, pushed the deputy aside, and charged the door.

"Freddy is here to rescue you again," the husband screamed.

"Maybe you and the baby need a place to stay—let him cool down. I could take you over to the Ramada."

"Why? He didn't do anything. I threw the bottle at him."

Freddy had one of his cards out. He wrote something down.

"Well, Liz, promise me that you will call me if there is a problem? It doesn't matter what time."

It was Freddy's standing offer to her, across all of the years. She took the card and looked up. Her eyes filled with tears.

"Eight years of marriage. And he is running around with that fucking spiderwoman."

Freddy smiled and met her eyes. She held his gaze. He watched her face, and wiped a tear from her cheek with his thumb.

FOURTEEN

The bridge was a gray place to live.

Even on the brightest day, you were struck by the dullness of the monstrosity. The New Jersey side of the big lady stuck her great, thick ankle into the water. The steel was exposed on that side. The New York ankle was booted with concrete. The shoe was visible at water level. Some people said the booted leg showed the city's dignity over New Jersey. No uptown lady would ever stick a bare toe in *that* muck.

On the Jersey side people didn't just dip a toe into the floating filth. Sometimes they actually dove in as recreation. As a young man, on the hottest day of the summer—on a day so hot you imagined you could smell the gray paint on the bridge boiling—young Freddy dove into the muck on a dare. He collected a dollar. Eventually, they joked, the river would wash off.

The Hudson River, at this point, wasn't even a real river. That was one of the great fables of New York. The Hudson was an estuary, filling with seawater running upstream. Only later did it meet a real freshwater river running downstate from West Point. Whatever it was—river or bay—life under the bridge was a gray life.

The job of painting the thing never ended. Painters came along, began painting the thing, worked every day for twenty years painting the thing, and then retired, having never finished. It was a perpetual job. Once the painters finished the monster they had to begin again at the other end. Rust was a killer. It could take down a bridge. This municipal screwup had just occurred on the other side of Manhattan with the Williamsburg Bridge. The city stopped painting that Erector set bridge for several years and it began to fall into the East River.

When a young man lives the bridge life, he knows bridge things. On Staten Island, where tolls and garbage fed secession talk every spring, they say toddlers learned to spell "Verrazano" before they learned to spell "dog" and "cat." See Spot run. See Spot jump. Off the bridge.

Yeah, there was that, too. Bridge life meant suicides. Someone was always threatening to jump. The threats snarled traffic. But if the cops got there, they usually talked the lunatics down. Still, a couple of times a year, some wack would jump. When they hit the water from that height, they tended to liquefy. That was the bridge life, too. "Bridge" meant life and death. Hell, on Staten Island, you could win drinks all night in the pubs by the ferry by naming the half-dozen people who had jumped off the Verrazano and survived. Two were cops. One was a guy who'd failed the police test.

Freddy Heflin lived a gray life. The bridge was always huge in his life, reminding him of his past, and what he could never be. Damn bridge. *Damn ear.*

The thought was there to bump into every night, every time he was alone. At the end of the terrible day, after being reminded that he was, at best, a hired baby-sitter, he came home and climbed out of his gun belt. He laid his gun on the used television and watched a phonograph needle drop on a piano concerto. Freddy Heflin was an anachronism. He was a guy who lived below one of the greatest goddamn bridges in the world but wanted to ford the river.

He looked out his window, troll-like, and checked to make sure the bridge was still there. He closed his lethargic eyes. Lilting music carried him off . . . *to the bubbles.*

He was underwater, again. It was 1975, and Paul Simon was singing "Kodachrome." The Doobie Brothers were still singing something about black water. In the water, Freddy hears nothing but his heart pounding. His cheeks puffed, he sees the sunken green Ford, nose down in the filth. He can see, he can always see well enough. He pulls open the door and sees a lily-white hand reaching to him from the driver's side. She is flowing but raven in the water. She is bent in the car. Her head is cut near her hairline. And there is an odd darkness in the foul water. Blood.

Freddy takes the girl in one arm, tight. It always happens. But the car tips heavily to the side and the exit is blocked, the door pinned to the ground. Freddy is wild in the eyes. Bubbles are bursting from his mouth. He is losing. He pulls, desperate, at the door. Nothing. His heart is a symphony of kettledrums. He begins to beat the side of his head and shoulders against the glass with the fury of being young, strong, healthy, and helpless. The glass cracks and bursts open with trapped air.

Liz is in young Freddy's arms again. A distant siren sounds.

Freddy awoke to a flashing red light in his driveway. The television was playing a blackjack infomercial. He got up from the couch and looked out the window. Bill Geisler jumped out of the police car and ran toward him.

FIFTEEN

The patrol car pulled into the driveway and Freddy stepped out. The old house was engulfed in flames. A real-life version of the fire engine on the sheriff's windowsill sprayed the trees feebly. The volunteer department might be able to save the next house.

"Did they find him?" the sheriff yelled. "Where's Gary?"

"Figs wasn't home," a fireman shouted back.

Two medics were on the lawn, working. Freddy saw a scorpion tattoo on a bare arm, and understood. His deputy, Geisler, frozen with fear, did not manage to speak beyond issuing the word "fire" during the ride over. Now he turned to face Freddy and found voice.

"She's in bad shape. Found her in the basement."

A fireman, holding a hose, pointed toward the Garrison water tower.

"If that tower still held water . . ." he said. "But we had no pressure."

Freddy looked past the medics as they worked on Monica, the girlfriend of Police Officer Gary Figgis. His eyes fluttered as he searched the scene.

"Where's Figs?" he repeated.

"On his way back from the city," Geisler said. "Cindy beeped him."

* * *

Moments later, a blue Chevy Citation swerved to a stop on the drive. The cops had barricaded the road, but this driver just made a sharp right turn and cut through a neighbor's driveway. Figs unfolded from his car, and stood, in shock. He studied the spectacle that had been his home and then noticed the crowd of rescue workers on his lawn. He ran over as Freddy stepped back to reveal Monica, on the ground. Figs knelt tearfully on the ground beside her. Tortured, he brushed back Monica's blood-clotted hair as she pushed the oxygen mask away.

"Baby," Figs said. "What were you doing in there?"

Monica spoke in a barely audible rasp. "Hey . . . I came to see you . . . I needed some, you know . . . I wanted to see you . . . but you weren't there . . ."

"I was working, baby."

The medics struggled to keep her on the oxygen, but she pushed it away, weakly. "I missed you . . . I went down to try and listen to the scanner . . . see if I could hear you . . . I nodded . . ."

The medics pressed the mask to her face. But she did not take another breath. They began to administer CPR. They pushed Figs away. Figs looked to Freddy then, his eyes wild and wet. He was furious and alone. They were one then, friend and sheriff.

Hours later Figs sat at Freddy's desk, filling out an accidental death report. There were half-eaten doughnuts, and eclairs, on the desk. Figs was eating his way through the despair. He nibbled his coffee cup. Cindy was making coffee. And not even bitching about it. They were all shaken that much into decency.

"The bastard is getting payback," Figs muttered.

"Who's that, Gary?" Cindy asked.

But Figs said nothing more. He looked out the window

into Garrison's main intersection and watched Ray Donlan pat Jack Rucker on the back. This concluded an apparently serious talk. Lagonda stood in the backup role, as always, smoking. Donlan crossed the street, walking toward him. Freddy was at Gary's shoulder then, watching.

"Lenny said it wasn't suspicious," Freddy said. "Said it was electrical."

Figs snorted. He was still watching Donlan, riveted and weighing, like a man watching a scale.

"Lenny is a freaking mechanic, Freddy," Figs said.

Donlan cracked open the door. "Figsy. I heard what happened."

Figs nodded, but avoided eye contact, much as the lieutenant had done the night before in the Four Aces.

"Look at me, Figsy."

Figs looked up. He was wet-eyed. Donlan softened his face when he saw the tears.

"Did you call in?"

"I am not in again until Tuesday."

"I'll call Lassaro myself," Donlan said. "Buy you a couple of weeks."

Figs did not say a word. Donlan smiled sadly at Freddy and then backed out of the door. Freddy looked to his friend with eyes that suggested, See, he isn't so bad. Figs sighed into the gaze. The sheriff's optimism about the town elder had become delusional.

"Yeah, whatever," he decided.

SIXTEEN

Freddy sat on the couch beside Cindy. Just then, in dungarees and T-shirts, they looked like any other couple in any other house on the riverbank. There were empty Chinese food containers on the table and a few bottles. Cindy had her head on the sheriff's shoulder as they watched television. Her eyes moved, and you saw that she was not dazed and glossy with the food and television.

The cop in Cindy Betts was working, always. And she was unsettled. "I don't know," she said. "I've been going through the violations and three quarters of the ones we write are against Jacksons, Johnsons, Browns, and Washingtons . . ."

Freddy watched the television. They were watching another cop show. Most of them seemed unreal. A white, blond, television cop pushed a black man against the wall. This was real enough.

"These aren't moving violations, Freddy," she said. "Seat belts. Insurance. Expired license. This is all stuff you can't tell until afterward—after you do the car stop."

"So?"

"So do you and Billy just pull over black people?"

"Cindy, we got a couple of nasty neighborhoods near us. Sometimes people—certain elements—drive through, take shortcuts to the bridge. I try and make it clear that if you cut through Garrison—you know—the cops there . . ."

"And if you're black . . ."

"And you fit a certain profile—then you are going to get pulled over."

Cindy shook her head with realization and sat up. She was working with the kind of cops in New Jersey they made movies about burying carloads of kids in Mississippi.

"You think *the men*—when they come home, across that bridge from a raging day in the city—want to find out that their front lawns have been turned into some kind of crack alley?"

"Oh, come on."

"What I'm saying is, this isn't racial."

Cindy poked her food, and nodded. But she did not believe. She was surprised, even by Freddy.

"Can we talk about something else?" he wanted to know.

Of course they could. Cindy Betts had heard enough. She was back in Elmira and the fields of Binghamton with the ignorant white prepubescent girls who believed that if you had sex with a black man you would have spotted kids that looked like Dalmatians or Holsteins. So, Cindy let Freddy sip his beer and watch his television. But suddenly, she was uneasy watching a cop show targeted for the fathers of cow pasture girls with a version of Police Officer Archie Bunker.

God, I am one of them.

SEVENTEEN

Figs was lying faceup in the Garrison holding cell. He had moved in, turning the former doctor's office, former tire storage area into his bedroom. He put a thin mattress and sheets on the cot. He had a razor and Aqua Velva at the foot of his bed. His gun belt and blue uniform hung from steel bars. Figs had another uniform in a plastic garbage bag.

"I carry *the Bag* in a garbage bag now," he announced in a dead tone on the morning after the fire, when he'd moved into the jail cell.

"Why don't you take a motel room?" Cindy asked before she left with Freddy.

"I wouldn't be comfortable," Figs said.

The phone rang, and kept ringing. Finally, he trudged out of the cell and answered the call.

"Yeah, dispatch. Uh-huh. Uh-hum. Well, tell them they can't, ma'am. Tell them just because they are television people doesn't mean they can park their van on your lawn. Or tell them you will never watch their station again. Is it Fox? Then turn them into *Eyewitness News.* Uh-huh. All right, then."

Figs walked to the window and looked out. Garrison was a cop carnival today. Freddy was in the middle of about five thousand of them. Many were already drunk and pissing in the street on the way to the funeral. Gary watched one cop holding his member in a white-gloved hand.

A couple of years ago, at a cop funeral on Long Island, the guys got completely screwed up. They were in line and gassed by the time the casket rolled out. When they broke ranks and ran to the bars to wait out the mass, some of them got really whacked. One knucklehead tried to shoot a bottle off the end of the bar. In turn, another young cop tried to shoot the badge off the shooter's uniform. Shots were fired, and a Member Of the Service was down *during* a police funeral. That was a new one, even for the NYPD.

The brass bitched about drinking in uniform. But this was Garrison, New Jersey, for Christ's sake. They weren't even licensed to carry in this state. And yet here they were, all carrying for a funeral. Who was going to say anything to a cop, in a cop's town at a cop's funeral? Everyone looked the other way. Figs returned to the jail cell for his uniform.

Freddy was in the middle of the street, managing the pavilion. Badge on his chest, gun on his hip, and scab on his nose, he directed traffic. The state cops and county cops were helping direct the New York cops around, too. Every cop within shooting distance chips in to help at a cop funeral. And God help the civilian who wanders into the tent. All of the cops chipping in have chips the size of One Police Plaza on their shoulders.

A black bricklayer and a Hispanic carpenter were working at Arby's. They looked on warily. A cop funeral, when you happen on it, is a frightening event. Every living cop is thinking about his own mortality and his family. The anger is simmering just beneath the uniform.

This was a full captain's funeral. So the cops would stand ten deep for a mile leading to the service. They snapped to attention as the funeral procession approached and a cop yelled over a bullhorn, "Detail, ready."

The thunder of the motorcycles would be heard. There would be at least twenty of them, slowly rumbling past. Sometimes the earth seemed to shake. The Garrison gathering was a grave-site service, different from the larger church service. Still, the police bagpipers, culled from the Emerald Society, would come, the drummers beating an ungodly, lonely beat. They would play "Amazing Grace." Then, perhaps the helicopters would do a flyover. Sometimes, the cops even had a riderless horse plod past.

Then came the cars and the black limousines and the gray hearse. Six uniformed pallbearers would be waiting. The cops in the funeral detail all wore skintight, white cotton gloves, polished brass buttons, and creased blue tunics. They hoisted the NYPD blue casket onto their uniformed shoulders and clicked into the church, synagogue, mosque, or cemetery. The widow, girlfriend, or mother followed, sometimes with fatherless children. If the mayor or governor had any grace, and they seldom did anymore, they did not call for the death penalty on the church grounds. They waited to do it at City Hall. Still, it was impossible to experience this scene and not get teary-eyed. Even the most twisted, vengeful, cynical reporters routinely cried at police funerals. Some of them even said it was the only time they felt alive covering a story.

Ordinarily, cops died too easily in a shootout. Sometimes, the dead cop didn't stand as a symbol to anything but senseless, and routine, mindless, violence. But this cop, like Glenn Tunney, had died for a cause. Superboy belonged to a nation of cops and law enforcement now. Or at least that was the way the police union was playing the suicidal death of Police Officer Murray Babitch in the media.

As the police funeral march began, Garrison was a rolling sea of blue. Once the mourners left the church, the families would move to the cemetery, on a hill overlooking the city and the river.

A line of limos rolled past filled with politicians who could not afford to miss any hero's funeral. Reporters could sort out the details later, but no mayor or borough president would miss the photo opportunity. Besides, New Jersey was closer than Suffolk County, Long Island. On this day, the mayor and union officials wanted to be seen together.

The cops talked quietly and laughed together. Many families, dressed in their Easter best, were strangers to Garrison. They hugged, slapped each other on the back, and whispered. Some passed notes. Cops who hadn't seen each other since the academy searched each other out. They gathered by precinct. This was truly a secret tribe.

Freddy and Cindy walked to the cemetery. A couple of cops whistled at her, but she held steady. They were as bad as construction workers. Freddy decided not to hear them.

Figs wandered out of the sheriff's office and was swallowed by the sweeping blue universe. He saw a familiar face. It happened at every funeral. "Hey, Charlie," he said.

But Charlie didn't respond. Figs looked away, hurt. Only Figs couldn't see the scarlet badge the union had pinned to his chest. Freddy and Cindy strolled past Frank Lagonda, his lard all shiny and blue, with a bouncy, big-haired blond. Only the most savage cops used a police funeral as an excuse to get laid. But it happened.

"Hello, Freddy," Lagonda said.

In a blue tent, Joey Randone escorted mourners to their assigned seats. As he led his wife, Liz, and their baby to their chairs, she moved stiffly. Her eyes darted to Freddy, who smiled back tenderly.

Rose Donlan, all blond and teetering on stick heels, stood smoking beneath a tree with several other first wives.

She wore sunglasses and a scarf, but a fresh bruise still showed on her cheek.

"Ray kept telling me we should prune the tree," Rose explained. "I was chasing this big dog off the lawn and *bam*—it hit me."

The first wives all smiled. They had all had similar dog problems.

Freddy was halfway up the hill when Ray Donlan grabbed him. He pulled him away from Cindy to PDA president Lassaro. The mayor was standing only a few feet away. The union boss wore the better suit.

"Vincent Lassaro, meet Sheriff Freddy Heflin."

Freddy held out his hand, beaming.

"Glad to meet you, Mr. Lassaro," he said. A lot of people said that to him, but Freddy even meant it.

"You people did a nice job, here. Real nice."

Across all the police funerals, and all the years, this was rote.

"Freddy is a helluva guy," Donlan continued. "He was trying to get on the Job for years with us. But he had this thing with his ears."

Freddy laughingly corrected him.

"No, it's just one ear. When I was a kid . . ."

An aide began to pull Lassaro away.

"Well, you should just call me, Freddy," Lassaro said. "You know it's rare when Ray Donlan puts his thumb in the air for a guy. Hey, it ain't the NYPD regular—but I got my own guys, you know? Call me, Freddy."

Lassaro moved off to his plastic seat. Donlan threw a fleshy arm around Freddy and grinned.

"Freddy, my boy, that is how things *happen*," he said.

EIGHTEEN

The cemetery was a large field of stones on top of a rolling hill. There were hundreds of stone markers with flags and emblems on stakes. All those societies and fraternities to join, and so little time. Neighbors called the place "Our Arlington." You could fill a detective squad with the dead cops buried in Garrison's Toro Hill Cemetery.

Sgt. Michael Lindsey, 1948–1976, "Heart of the 38th."
Tony Caastanza, NYPD, 1954–1981, "Sixteen years of service."
Officer Gary Matursky, NYPD, 1951–1979, "In the line of duty."

There was one marker, a newer one, that everyone made sure to pass. The headstone was extravagant and surrounded by flowers. Many laid there today, too.

Officer Glenn Tunney, NYPD, 1960–1994, "Martyr to the system. Hero to his peers."

Cop funerals made terrific television. Even regular ones. But this was extraordinary television happening.

"Glenn Tunney," one reporter said, standing by the cop's

grave. "He was murdered in his cell while waiting for the
Grand Jury to decide his fate. Two years later—déjà vu."

It wasn't exactly the same story, but hey, this was television. The camera swung from the TV reporter doing the
stand-up to a big blue tent in the background.

"Another hero cop," the reporter continued, "this one
dubbed 'Superboy.' Unwilling to trust the system that destroyed his friend, he leaped to his death."

A winch lowered the coffin into the ground. A safe distance from the weeping, Freddy and Cindy watched the
ceremony from an access road. Cindy, ever the cop, leaned
to Freddy.

"What's in there?"

"Uniform," Freddy replied.

Liz Randone and Rose murdered each other with their
eyes on the receiving line with Babitch's mother. Every cop
told the grieving mother the same thing: Don't you worry
about a thing, Ma. We are all your sons now.

As the orchestrated, and entirely false, police lament
finished, the bagpipers played on.

NINETEEN

The late afternoon sunlight filled the sheriff's office. The cops were emptying out of the town. They left behind a couple of dozen handkerchiefs, and countless cigarette packs, beer bottles, and broken sunglasses. Police officers are world-class litterbugs. They like to leave their mark on a place after a funeral. The cops from Long Island and Staten Island felt especially free to dirty up a town in New Jersey, the carcinogenic state. So as the town sanitation workers filled their bags, and the cemetery workers filled in the grave, the cops went on with their work.

Freddy Heflin was feeling electric, charged with "The Blue Day," as he heard it called, and his half promise of a job from the PDA president, Lassaro. He felt like a Thanksgiving balloon from the Macy's parade, and floated down the main street of Garrison on the way over to his office.

But when he entered his office, the balloon burst. The Internal Affairs cops from New York City were already sitting around his desk. Moe Tilden studied the frames on the wall; he was particularly interested in the yellowed story of Freddy's heroic rescue of Liz Randone. Tilden sat politely waiting, hat in hand, on a stool near Freddy's desk. Carson, occasionally taking out a notebook to scribble in, wandered around the office.

"Hey, how you doing," Tilden said. He was holding a file

in his hands. Without waiting for Freddy to respond, he opened it as the sheriff sat down. Traditionally, Internal Affairs tended to be short on pleasantries. They did not need a formal invitation, either, to begin working.

Freddy sat down at his desk and examined a folder of 8- by 10-photos. He thumbed through a picture of Murray Babitch and Ray Donlan. The lieutenant looked quite dapper. As Freddy weighed the photographs, Moe Tilden fingered a travel case of Freddy's cassette tapes. Handwritten on the spines of the boxes were *Preludes and Fuges, 1957; Sonata I, 1958; Sonata II, 1959.* Tilden was frankly surprised by the cop's taste. He figured the only opera Freddy ever listened to was *Tommy.*

"I didn't think they allowed classical music in Jersey," Tilden said. Freddy ignored his visitor. He stared at a photograph of Donlan and an unknown man standing together, talking animatedly.

"Who is this?" Freddy asked.

Carson was leaning against a wall, thumbing through one of Freddy's paperback crime novels. His reading tastes were not so classical. Freddy preferred *The Choir Boys* and *The Onion Field* over *Crime and Punishment.* Carson looked up from *Prince of the City* when he heard Freddy's question.

"Tony Torillo. You heard of him?"

Freddy nodded. He put the open folder on his desk. A picture of Babitch stared back up at him.

"Look," he said, pointing. "This guy was well liked here. Sometimes he'd stop by for drinks with the boys. But I don't know anything about him—"

"You knew Ray Donlan was his uncle," Carson said, interrupting. If the IA investigator was a fighter, he would be all jab and no knock-out punch, Freddy decided.

"I knew that. And that he was some kind of hero."

Carson tapped the yellowed newspaper article on the sheriff's wall. "Like you."

Tilden crossed to the window and lit a cigarette. The last of the crowd was dispersing. Men in blue and their families. Ordinarily, he knew cops didn't bring their wives and kids to funerals. This rarely happened out in Nassau County, Long Island. He watched the last of the TV crews depart. Idiots, drawn to the TV lights like moths, slowly disappeared.

Tilden was something of a Revolutionary War buff. He knew that not far from here a rented army had once camped. They were all hired hands. "I don't know how you do it, Sheriff," Tilden said. "Keeping all these Hessians in line."

Carson snapped the pack of photos off Freddy's desk. He flipped through them, staring mutely back at grinning cops and their families.

"All blue," Tilden continued. "Everyone packing a gun. All together. One door down from the next. Wives borrowing sugar. Husbands borrowing Teflon-coated bullets. You are the sheriff of Cop Land."

"Excuse me?"

"You're the sheriff of Cop Land."

Tilden smiled. He was pleased with himself and the title. "Cop Land" would look a lot better than "Garrison" painted across the spent water tower. Carson, still shuffling through the photos, paused at one of Ray Donlan and Freddy. He held it up so Tilden could view it. The lieutenant nodded. Freddy shifted, uncomfortably.

"See, Sheriff," Tilden continued, "I have a sticky problem. My jurisdiction ends—in a sense—at the George Washington Bridge. But some of the men I watch live beyond that bridge—where no one is watching."

Tilden snorted to himself with the realization that he

was a one-eyed cop talking to a one-eared sheriff about cop surveillance. They were blind and dumb to wrongdoing.

"I'm watching," Freddy insisted.

Tilden met his eyes and held them, measuring the sheriff. His gaze was respectful but searching.

"I can see that. Your crime rate here is—"

"The lowest in northern Jersey," Freddy interrupted.

"Yet you got Newark there—and Hoboken over there, and Jersey City," Carson said.

"We do a good job."

"With a staff of three," Tilden said. "No. What you have here is a town that scares the shit out of certain people."

"This is like that television show," Carson said. "Who is that guy—Barney Fife?"

"Hey," Freddy insisted, "I told you. I'm watching. I mean, do you see these guys wearing silk shirts and driving fancy cars? This isn't like one of those towns in the Dominican Republic where the dealers who sell crack in New York City live. These guys are not dirty like that. No. Their swimming pools—they're aboveground." The sheriff paused a full beat. "You know," he continued, "you raise your family somewhere decent and that's a crime now?"

Tilden smiled and nodded to Carson. The lieutenant was asking to be left alone with Freddy Heflin. Carson grabbed his coat and walked into the outer office. Figs entered with a fresh pack of cigarettes and saw the Internal Affairs investigator. Carson smiled, but Figs just glared back at him. Tilden closed the door to Freddy's office. They were alone together now, just two cops talking.

"So we buried a shoe today," Tilden said. "We buried a freaking shoe. And that doesn't bother you?"

Freddy didn't look at him. He set his jaw before he spoke.

"He jumped off the GWB."

Tilden shook his head. "But his body never hit the water, Freddy."

Tilden lit another cigarette. His only chance was to find a cop's heart buried somewhere in Sheriff Freddy Heflin's uniform.

"And that doesn't bother you, Freddy? What does? That I investigate other cops? You're a man who always pined to be a cop."

"I am a cop," Freddy insisted.

"A city cop . . . A member of the NYPD. Three appointments with the health board in three years. Appeals of hearing tests. You may be in *law enforcement*, Freddy. But you are not a 'cop.'"

Freddy stiffened against the insult but said nothing.

"Now, I may watch cops," Tilden continued. "But—tell me if I am wrong—every day out of these windows so do you."

Across the street Ray Donlan and the others were gathering. In a huddle, Jack Rucker and Randone conversed with Lagonda.

"You watch cops, too. And because we're both in law enforcement, we share a duty. Where there's a stink, we must investigate. We must gather evidence. Because evidence makes us see the truth. Is this the stink of a criminal act? Or is it a turd in a bag? Every day I see cops who lost their way. And I can tell you that these lost cops are the minority. Still, they tend to gather. They can be family men, heroes. They can have their reasons. But they are also the cops who bring the cases down. Addicted cops. Cops who lie and look the other way. Cops who plant. Cops who beat. Cops who take. Cops who kill. Their ambivalence is contagious. They're like maggots. Where you find one, you often find the next. Now, I don't like this. I went to the same fucking academy with that guy out there. I stood by Ray Donlan at graduation. He was a beauty. A real collar man. And to the cop he was—to his memory—I am loyal. But through the fog of loyalty to *the men*—men of *the department*—the evidence makes me see. And these days what I see is like an island just out of my reach. I see this beautiful island shining through this fog—every house financed by one of two mob banks—uh-huh, that's right, Sheriff—what I see is your town."

Freddy shook his head, in complete denial. Tilden took a deep drag on his cigarette. Outside, Donlan and his buddies began to disperse, some climbing into cars and driving off. The others disappeared into the Four Aces Tavern.

"Listen to me, Sheriff," Tilden said. "Babitch ain't dead. You know it. I know it. Ray got him off that bridge—alive. Before he could talk. Ray wasn't so lucky the last time with Glenn Tunney when the shit hit. That one he had to take care of later in Tunney's jail cell. He had to pay an inmate."

Freddy jerked as if rear-ended. He was overwhelmed by the information.

"But now what," Tilden said, "what does Ray do this time? That is the sixty-four-thousand-dollar question."

Lieutenant Moe Tilden wiggled his fingers in the air. He was reaching for something just out of his grasp. Freddy watched him do it and thought of the car door he had reached all those years ago under the water.

"That's why I want your help, Freddy. Because you are *inside*. Because—besides the church traffic and the cats in the trees—there isn't much here for you, is there? I look at you and I see a man waiting for something *to do*. And here I stand, here I stand saying, *Sheriff, I have something for you to do*."

Tilden drove his cigarette butt into the sheriff's idiotic, gun-shaped ashtray, and moved to the door. He slammed it shut as Figs, on the stoop, looked to Freddy knowingly.

TWENTY

Early the next day, Freddy Heflin sat in his Garrison patrol car watching Gary Figs at the water's edge. Now, with the city cop's words coursing through his brain—the sound of human conscience—the sheriff watched another funeral service. Cop Land, as Tilden had called it, might have been a million miles away. The great city, like the great bridge, was gray on the horizon.

Figs was staring at a muted pile that used to be his own passion. Monica filled an urn now. He stood at the water's edge with slumped shoulders. He was sadder than any cop had looked the day before in Garrison. He scattered ashes from a purple urn on the water. The tattooed girl fell silent and gray to the water.

Later, they drove through Garrison. Sunday in Garrison was a postcard come to life. Several men were playing softball as wives and children stood around cheering. Freddy was driving. As he passed people, they stared curiously at his passenger, Gary Figs. The cop was grubby and despondent. He might have been any EDP—emotionally disturbed person, as the cops called them over the radio—on any block in the city. It was a good thing, too, the people of Garrison could not hear *their* neighbor. The cynical cop was singing the theme song to *Mister Rogers* as the town passed by his window. *Would you be mine—Could you be mine—Won't you be—my neighbor?* Figs continued to stare straight ahead, red-eyed and dead to society. Freddy watched his passenger warily. He drove through the madness that their lives had become.

"You know, you don't have to sleep in the cell at the station, Gary. You can stay in my basement—till you find a new place."

Every year had its "in" car; these days they were four-wheel-drive vehicles. The rambling four wheelers, Freddy realized, were particularly hot on the East Coast. This was the kind of useless detail that highway cops and town sheriffs knew. Those cops were the first to realize American trends as they barreled past the speed checkpoint. *Oh, yeah, America is happening in front of me. Ten years ago I was writing tickets on Pintos every day. Volkswagons ten years before that. Pontiac GTOs and Mustangs before that. My father was a cop, too. He liked to brag that he wrote up '57 Chevys. He was a Chevy Nomad man himself, too. My grandfather was a cop, too. He liked to brag that he wrote a taillight on an Edsel once. Last year, I was writing Grand Cherokees. In Detroit, I'd heard cops say the police were only ticketing foreign-built cars.*

A purple-red Suzuki Tracker—this year's big car among the drug dealers from New York City to Newark—thumped past blasting rap music from boom box speakers. The song, one celebrating the new ghetto crime, home invasion robberies, split the calm easiness of the Garrison afternoon. Ice-T was not a welcome guest in Cop Land. Boom boxes were outlawed here. So were black teenagers.

Suddenly the softball team with guns couldn't hear themselves screaming support for each other. A collective sneer passed over the face of the white team. Donlan,

Rucker, Lagonda, Crasky, and the rest of the town team were moved by the loud interruption. The game shuddered to a halt as they put down their baseball mitts and beers. Some held their bats tighter as the Tracker thundered past them.

The black teenagers in the four-wheel-drive Suzuki may as well have been in a lone Japanese zero fighter wandering into Pearl Harbor the day after the infamous sneak attack. Cindy watched from the sheriff's office as the Tracker roared by her post. Several cars of white guys—she recognized them as the cop townies—gave chase, honking their horns. The scene smelled of fear and revenge. Concerned, she stood and fastened her holster.

A few blocks down, the revenge caravan passed the Caldor parking lot as Freddy and Figs emerged from the store. They saw the speeding car, filled with black faces, followed by the cars filled with drunken white faces and understood the seriousness of the chase completely. This was a *situation*—a version of the fabled racial attacks in Howard Beach and Bensonhurst—as bad as anything that happened on the other side of the river in the race war in Crown Heights.

Freddy moved to his squad car quickly. Figs moved, too, with the quickened importance of a peacemaker.

The chase ended in a suburban cul-de-sac marked DEAD END. No advertisement for Jersey had ever carried a more truthful message. Nearly rolling over, the Tracker screeched to a stop. Two teenagers sat inside, terrified. Music continued to pound. The off-duty cops emerged from their cars and homes in green-and-red uniforms, holding baseball bats. It was like a ten-thirteen—Officer Needs Assistance—had been broadcast through some underground town speaker system. The kids' stereo, although certainly loud, was no match. A younger kid in the car, wearing a backward Knicks cap, was brave enough to stammer.

"Jesus Christ," he screeched at the cocked gun that now was the town of Garrison, New Jersey, pointed at his head. "We ain't doing shit! We just going to Action Park!"

Cindy was growing equally brave. She moved through a circle of men, pausing beside Rucker. Lagonda was already rifling through the Suzuki glove compartment.

"Okay, where's the piece? You got a gun in here?" he said. It wasn't really a question. And then, "If I stick myself on a hypo, you are going to catch a major beating."

"Homey don't play that," one kid replied.

"Look in their pockets," Rucker commanded Cindy.

"I can't do that. I didn't pull them over. I don't have probable cause to search."

"We are your probable cause, honey. What do you want, a letter from the attorney general?"

"I told you—we going to Action Park," the kid said.

"Action park is in Vernon," Lagonda said.

"This is all the action and park you are going to see, homey," one of the cops yelled from behind him.

No one was laughing.

Freddy stepped out of his car and slammed the door. He was wearing his sunglasses, but the tenseness showed in his face. Figs did not get out of the car. He was holding his plastic Caldor bag tightly.

"Look in their pockets, Freddy," Rucker ordered.

"First of all, fellas," the sheriff told the kids, taking off his glasses, "turn off the music."

There was hestitation.

"Do it."

One of the kids had the sense to snap off the radio. The second Garrison police car pulled up. Bill climbed out, Cindy watching intently. Just what was Freddy Heflin capable of doing to the kids, anyway, in the name of law and order in Garrison?

"Get out of the car," the sheriff said. "Get out now."

"I think I smell something," Joey Randone said.

"Look in their pockets, Freddy," Rucker said. "Now."

The kids stood next to each other, silent and blinking against the fear.

"Search 'em, Freddy."

"Now—um—I want you fellows to tell these men that you're sorry for messing up their weekend."

Cindy, incredulous, looked at Freddy. Bill stepped up beside her, watching. The Garrison Sheriff's Department had the presence to handle this in an entirely different way. But Freddy was the boss. They waited one full beat, then two. The kids would not utter a public act of contrition.

"Look in their pockets, Freddy," Rucker repeated.

"This is *whack*," the kid said.

"Do what I said," Freddy tried again.

The kids stayed their position, tight-lipped. Perhaps they even believed they were in New Jersey, protected by the Constitution, whatever that was. They hadn't seen any sign getting off the bridge that had read LAST STOP IN AMERICA. But this was the cops' ground. Screw the cliché stuff about a cop's backyard. This was their *front* yard, their driveway. At last, Jack Rucker strode forward, shaking his head.

"This is very cute, Freddy. But you have cause and I want to get on with my day. Tell them to put their hands on the fucking car."

This was no longer a suggestion. But Freddy stood, his face like the stone of a marker in the cemetery on the hill.

Rucker went into his police-command mode. "Hands on the car. HANDS ON THE CAR!"

The kids complied with the order, and spread their appendages to be searched. Rucker rummaged through their pockets. Freddy rocked on his feet, brooding. Rucker came out of the kids' pockets with a bluntie and a bag of pot.

A moment later, Freddy shuffled to his car. He was followed by the rest of the Garrison police force, Cindy and Bill, as well as the two kids, in cuffs. As they reached the car, Randone and Rucker moved past. They spoke in mocking voices, ones they believed to be an impression of the dopey town sheriff:

"I want you to tell these men you're sorry for ruining their weekend."

"Didn't you know that Bluntie was loaded, son?"

Rucker wanted to know. "Just what the fuck do we pay you for, Freddy?"

Freddy had lit a cigarette during the illegal search. He stamped it out and held eye contact with Rucker and Randone as they passed. He climbed into his squad car, embarrassed and angry.

Later that night Freddy sat in the Four Aces Tavern. He was in the same place but was no longer the same part of it. He sucked on a cigarette and stared at the television. The station showed some footage from Babitch's funeral. For a moment, Freddy appeared on the screen. He shuffled out of the picture. He was definitely out of the picture now. There were a few cops in the back. It was even festive. Donlan and company were decidedly absent. On the television the mayor spoke.

"This reminds us of the blue line that separates us from anarchy. That's why I am forming a bipartisan commission to study the working conditions of the police in our city."

The after-work conditions at the Four Aces were frothy and foulmouthed. Another politician's head and face filled the screen.

"If that officer hadn't jumped, the mayor would be talking about *increasing* supervision."

Freddy shrugged with the weight of the argument. He turned to find his deputy filling the doorway.

"We got a call about this thing up at Ray Donlan's. Maybe you should come, boss."

TWENTY-ONE

The lights and the loud music snapped off as Jack Rucker carried a cake with a single candle through the small crowd. It was the same crowd that gathered in the precincts, in bars, and at funerals. But now their faces shone with light and victory.

" 'Happy birthday to you,' " they sang.

He was three days old. Murray Babitch did not have an identity yet. He still had his badge in his pocket, not that it meant what it had meant a week ago. As going-away parties went, this gathering was a perverse one. Superboy, having been buried the previous day, was now going to disappear into the cop witness protection program. Whatever that meant. Wherever that led. He sat in the middle of the group as they carried the cake through his uncle's house, and then stood, grinning. He was wearing a stupid coned party hat. The cop did have that happy toddler's smile and the crowd applauded him. He blew out the single candle.

"Congratulations, Murray," one cop said.

"He's not Murray anymore," another cop said. "He is Mortimer Snerk of Tempe, Arizona."

"That's right," the cop replied. "Whoops, Mr. *Snerdly*. But didn't they already make this movie—*My Blue Heaven*? Murray is the Henry Hill of cops, and he didn't even rat out his goodfellas."

Everyone laughed. Someone in the back turned the stereo back on. Frank Sinatra boomed across the room. Frank made the going-missing party a Jersey thing. Babitch bent over and kissed a pretty woman. There was a collection of them.

"This is kind of cool, you know," Murray Babitch said. "Not many people get to lead *two* lives."

With the room happily drunk and sated, Ray Donlan walked upstairs and into his bedroom. His gait was plodding, even unsure. He dialed the number. He spoke into the phone while holding his head, so quietly that Vince Lassaro could barely hear him. He did not see his wife, Rose, eavesdropping in the doorway. It was a rookie mistake to let her that close. On the street, these were the mistakes that got cops killed.

"I don't want to go through this again," Ray said. "I can't. I told the boys—I mean—they're downstairs now, saying good-bye."

"So, fine, let them say good-bye," Lassaro said.

Both of them knew that Glenn Tunney never got to say good-bye. He killed a kid and then threatened to save his own life by talking to the prosecutors about the union. They had been trying to make a racketeering case against the union for years. Lassaro could not afford that. None in the PDA could stand the attention. Ray had to hire an inmate to kill the cop in his cell.

"I can't go through this again."

Suddenly a shadow played across his bed. Ray Donlan looked up, scared. Rose stood in the doorway. Donlan catalogued his mistake and looked across the room to Rucker. They both looked uneasy with the pending task.

"Vince, I—"

"Who is Vince?" Lassaro asked, calmly. He was not a

fool to be wiretapped so easily. "What phone line are you
on?"

"A clean one. It's wired through Leo's garage."

"Look," Lassaro said in the same tone Jack Rucker had
used with the black kids they'd captured that afternoon.
"You tell me the IAD should lose this file—you tell me you
want this rat fuck Tilden off your back—and I am telling
you that can happen, you were brilliant the other night, brilliant. They got nothing on you other than Superboy. Now, I
can back them off, Ray, but you gotta tell me that boy's body
will wash up. We are all dead if he doesn't."

"Vince, this is my sister-in-law's kid."

The union boss waited to speak again. He never mis-
placed useful information.

"Didn't you say he was adopted?"

Rose Donlan had a brave, cunning heart. And whatever position she found herself in now had been set in motion by
her husband's own wretched, cheating excess. Hers was not
a passion to be trifled with, or easily discarded. She seldom
admitted it to strangers, but her favorite scene in a movie,
the one she identified with the most, was the baptism scene
from *The Godfather*. She liked the idea of whacking out all
of your enemies and using the church as your alibi. Rose
looked up, tense, as someone entered the downstairs bathroom. She wrote a message on a paper bar napkin with a
Sharpie marker.

As the music thundered from the Donlan home through the
neighborhood, Freddie moved his patrol car into the driveway. He counted a dozen cars in the street. As he got out,
he slammed his door. He could see through the windows
that the party was packed. No one heard his car. The deputy

started to get out of the car, too, but Freddy waved him back.

As Freddy approached the door, Lagonda burst out with his big-haired girlfriend.

"Hey, Frank," Freddy said. "Is Ray in there?"

"Need him to turn it down?"

"I need to talk to Ray."

As music throbbed and oozed out, Freddy moved to the door. Frank sighed. He released his girlfriend's hand and moved past Freddy. "Stay here," he commanded.

Lagonda slithered into the house and Freddy caught a glimpse of Rose Donlan and some other familiar faces through the door. As Freddy shifted his weight, Lagonda's girlfriend spiked her way over to the squad car and put a finger on her lips. Bill smiled. On the subways they called guys like Bill Vic, as in victim.

"Your guys' guns. Are they the same ones they use in the city?"

"We have .38 specials here."

"They got bigger, faster guns in the city," she said. "Glocks." The woman knew her shapes and sizes.

Ray Donlan emerged from the throng, looking haggard and preoccupied. He would not look directly at Freddy. He shouted at someone to turn down the music.

"What's up, Freddy?" he asked. "You want me to turn it down?"

"Well. It is after midnight. The town has school to-morrow."

"LOU. TURN IT DOWN. NO, DOWN."

The music evaporated. Lagonda started to head out again with his girlfriend.

"Frank, don't go yet," Donlan said, reaching.

Freddy spoke again. "Ray," he said. "This doesn't make sense."

"I gotta take Donna home," Lagonda interrupted.

Donlan smiled tersely.

"Take her to the train."

Lagonda understood the urgency in the boss's eyes. He moved off, shaking his head. Donlan watched him go, then turned back to Freddy, trying to ease him with a smile.

"This don't make things very easy for me," Freddy said. "I mean, this is a big thing you are having. On a school night. The day after. I mean . . ."

"Freddy, what are you talking about?"

The sheriff winced. "Ray. This guy—from IAD, Moe Tilden—he came to see me yesterday. He's got pictures of you—"

"Freddy," Donlan interrupted. "That guy has had a hard-on for me for years. It's a personal thing. He's a scumbag. You know how they recruit at IAD. They catch you on the take and they tell you you can either do the time or join them."

"Well. He knows—you know—that Superboy . . ."

Donlan said nothing. He looked at Freddy, unblinking, as if he had two heads. Or worse, as if Freddy was high on smack, waterlogged with heroin. He did not know if Freddy was wired or not. And he wasn't going to have a conversation played back to him, ever.

"And what did you say, Freddy?"

"I told him that Superboy was dead," Freddy continued. "I told him he was wrong about you. But Ray, I am the sheriff. I am supposed to know what is going on. *How do you think this looks?*"

"Go home, Freddy. And don't think so much. I heard what happened today with Jack and the boys. I'm sorry about that. Everyone is very high-strung."

"Ray, I can't—"

"Go home, Freddy. Go home."

It was not a suggestion. The lieutenant gave the sheriff his order and then turned, closing the door on him.

Ray Donlan entered the party but missed his wife talking to the cop. Rose was holding a drink pressed oddly in a party napkin. She saw the cop she wanted in the hallway. Rose pressed the drink into the hand of Murray Babitch. At first the cop resisted.

"I'm fine, Aunt Rose. *I am.*"

"*But, Murray,*" she said, winking, "I want you to have this."

She continued to watch him even as he walked away. Perplexed, Babitch took the drink into the bathroom with him.

TWENTY-TWO

Freddy was still shaking with indecision when he came
home to his empty, soundless house. After a few minutes he
filled his world again with classical decision. He was leaning
on a speaker, studying a beat-up album cover. On the ancient turntable, Glenn Gould's song was drifting through
the house. It was one of his favorites, from the *Goldberg
Variations* album.

The themes in Freddy's life were coarser. He was partially deaf, not blind. And as he stood there in his apartment, he could see he was a flawed hero at best, and maybe
much worse. The burdens of loyalty and disloyalty weighed
upon him even more than usual.

He unbuttoned his shirt and sat back on his couch,
smoking. As headlights sprayed across his living room, he
sat. He did not expect any visitor, friend or foe, at this late
hour. He went to the door and opened it. Liz Randone stood
there, drowning in runny mascara and defeat.

"Hi."

"Hi."

Liz was obviously nervous. She had a coat thrown over
her shoulder. She was holding two packs of cigarettes.

"Uh," she said.

Freddy was helpful but cautious.

"You get in another fight?"

"We were gonna have 'the big talk.' "

"Uh-huh."

Liz started to weep. "I had my mom take Caroline. But Joey calls and says he's stuck. That he made some arrest— and that—"

Liz descended into bawling. It was not any easier to watch her drown this time either, Freddy realized.

"I mean, I can't believe him anymore when he tells me something."

Freddy looked about nervously as a car passed by. It was impossible for anyone passing his lighted porch at this hour not to recognize Freddy and Liz. Garrison held no secrets.

"I mean, the man is a liar. Our marriage has no *credibility*."

That was a strange word to use to describe a union, but one she had learned from watching Geraldo talk about O.J. for three years. But she was right. The Randone marriage failed on that issue alone, Freddy realized. The town failed on that issue, too. Liz pulled herself out of her emotional tailspin and managed an enchanting smile.

"So, I decided to get drunk," Liz continued. "And I remembered this bottle of—that you gave us when we got married."

Freddy remembered too. "Sambuca," he said.

"And it tasted like licorice. It made me want to smoke. So I went out and got cigarettes. And as I was driving by your house—"

"Liz," Freddy said, helping her. "You want to come inside?"

Liz smiled, oddly. She was sad with embarrassment and self-delusion. She nodded like a little girl. She wondered: Is it fair to want him so?

*   *   *

The cops were emptying out of Ray Donlan's house. The music was low now. Glenn Gould would have worked in this tired room. But Ray Donlan did not understand or possess anything classical. There were only two kinds of music this cop had any use for: loud, and louder. Loud music was something you played when you wanted to make sure no one was listening to your conversation. Louder music was the sound to cheat on your wife to. Ray headed into the kitchen and looked back once to see the cops bidding a strange adieu to Superboy.

"Take care. Put this behind you."

"Yeah, even put you behind you."

"I will," Babitch said. "Thanks to Ray."

Murray Babitch bear-hugged the cops at the door. Still uneasy, Rose headed up the stairs to her bedroom.

"Take care Mur—I mean, Pete."

"You have a great life," one cop said.

"You too, Mike," Babitch replied.

"Send us some—I don't know—what's even in Georgia anyway?"

"Peaches."

"Well," the cop said on his way out, "send us some of those."

The rest of the cops were leaving. But suddenly, like an iceberg, Rucker floated in front of Babitch, who was tipsy with beer and emotion.

"Ray wants to see you out back."

"Tell him fifteen minutes," Superboy replied.

Rucker narrowed his eyes until he looked absolutely jagged. But he relented, realizing that there were only a couple of cops left.

"What? Tell him fifteen. I am saying my good-byes here."

Rucker was pissed, but rage was a permanent condition with him, anyway. He boiled off into another room.

"They taking you away tonight, Mur?" one last cop asked.

"I guess so," Babitch said, realizing.

Freddy and Liz sat on the couch. It was easier and more exciting than Freddy would have believed possible. He imagined he could feel her pulse just sitting next to her. They were smoking and sipping drinks. Music played softly. The television was on, but mute.

"This is pretty scratchy, Freddy. You can get CDs—you know—in stereo now."

"Wouldn't matter to me."

Liz blinked, touching her own ear. She smiled.

"Oh, right."

"Isn't he great. He played like that—so fast—without even looking at the keys."

"Like Ray Charles."

"Yeah. Everyone thought he was a genius. But he just stopped doing concerts after that. 'Cause he couldn't get it perfect, you know."

The music was building. So was Freddy. The sheriff conducted the concerto with his hands. Sometimes, he did this when he was directing traffic. But there were never enough cars passing to make his baton waving anything more than the crude version of the art that it was.

"Oh." Liz watched him with wonder. She was quite buzzed and barely listening. She was fascinated with him, not the music. She touched his ear. "Which one is it?" she asked.

Freddy smiled and tried to focus on the music. He almost wished Liz would join him.

"The other one," he said. Freddy pointed to the album in

his hands, saying, "Beethoven was completely deaf at the end—you know—of his career. Gould had this funky ear, too. See? He was a goofy-looking guy. But he was a genius, you know."

Liz sat up. Suddenly she realized why she and Freddy connected with the troubled genius's music. They were damaged things collecting other damaged things. Some people collected toys, Freddy collected flaws. She leaned on his shoulder, dreamily. Freddy stiffened. She turned and put her lips close to Freddy's bad ear. Then she whispered, "You smell good."

"Hmm?"

Liz smiled sweetly. Freddy was deaf to her affection. Liz was a bit amazed by herself. Betrayal was not as difficult as she'd imagined.

"Oh, nothing."

Freddy blushed. He was unsure what to say in response to what he hadn't heard.

"You know, it's a funny thing when you owe someone your life."

Freddy shrugged. Then nodded. Liz touched his cheek.

"Why is it you never married again?" she wanted to know.

Freddy turned and looked into her eyes. Unlike the river, they were bottomless.

"All the best girls got taken."

Tears dropped from Liz's cheek. They made a faint sound as they fell on the record cover in her hands. Freddy reached over and wiped her cheek. The silence between them grew until they were overcome with passion and memory. Freddy saw himself leaning over her prone body all those years ago and breathing life into the drowning girl.

Now, as Glenn Gould, the flawed man, played on, they tenderly kissed. They were soft, then sweet kisses. His quickened, running across her cheek, neck, forehead, and hair. Together again, for the first time. They arrived at a forbidden place, and felt like guilty schoolkids behind a tree.

Suddenly, Liz backed away, self-conscious and unwilling.

She put the back of her hand to her mouth and gasped. "Uh. This is crazy."

Freddy looked at her longingly, but did not argue.

"This isn't me," Liz said.

And she was gone before the song had ended.

Murray Babitch was too drunk now to even stand and urinate correctly. He placed the drink on the bathroom counter and regained his balance. The note hung like a billboard around the oversized drink. The cop splashed water on his face. He rose, looking in the mirror, and blinked. Any sobriety he felt was an invention. Still, he noticed the note reflected in the mirror, then peeled it off the drink. He read the scrawl and looked back in the mirror, instantly terrified. He thought suddenly of Glenn Tunney. He wondered if anyone had warned him.

There were coats and holstered guns hanging on a shower rod. He grabbed a revolver and stuffed it into his pants. As he flushed Rose's warning away, the blood in his cheeks drained, too. So Ray was going to kill another cop. Not him. Not this time. Murray Babitch was no Glenn Tunney, after all.

Superboy was acutely forewarned and forearmed. The cop was *live* now, or as the kids in the car had shouted just before he shot them, "We live now. All the way live."

Murray Babitch walked outside. Every sense was alive to the danger. He thought briefly of those Spiderman comics he used to read and how the webbed one always tasted danger: "My Spider senses are tingling . . ." Superboy was electric—make that NYPD electric blue. He stood at the backdoor, shaken.

Donlan came out of the darkness. He stood at the back of his aboveground pool, smoking. The tower rose, wooden and barren behind him. Babitch looked at the tower and then bounded down the steps. He stumbled and approached the covered pool. He spoke to Donlan from the opposite side of the pool, terrified.

"You know, Ray. It's a great thing you did. Making a place. Where the men could stick together, you know?"

Donlan nodded, grim with his task. Smoke eerily escaped from him.

"I mean," Babitch continued, "you didn't have to do this for me—I mean, you coulda just . . ."

He swallowed the rest of the sentence with a shrug. By then, Jack Rucker was at the backdoor. Frank Lagonda joined him. Donlan and Babitch stood together now as they had stood together on the same lawn following Murray's graduation from the police academy.

"I always told Ma, 'Uncle Ray, he doesn't like me very much.'"

"I always liked you," Ray said, smiling. "You just sweat too much."

Babitch smiled wider still, painfully wider. Donlan nodded to Rucker, who looked to Lagonda for help.

"Everyone is gone?" he asked his accomplice.

Lagonda nodded solemnly. Rucker relayed this information to Donlan with a nod.

"So," Babitch asked, "what is gonna happen? We meeting some people? I am pretty buzzed. I mean, I am all packed and everything, but . . ."

He noticed Rucker and Lagonda approaching him from behind.

"But," he continued, "maybe we should wait and do this tomorrow or something."

Rucker and Lagonda smiled sadly at Babitch. Only a few days before they were ready to do anything *for* a fellow cop, and had. Now they were ready to do anything *to* Murray Babitch.

"Where's Joey?" Murray asked. Randone should have been there, too, Murray decided. Maybe Joey was sneaking up on him.

"Working tonight," Lagonda answered.

Babitch nodded. He was an absolute prisoner of paranoia and fear. Donlan sucked on a cigarette, devoid of voice and hollow of soul.

"I'm sorry it had to come out this way, Murray."

Babitch shrugged and lowered his eyelids. "Oh, it's not so bad, Jack." Donlan looked to Rucker, who put his hand on top of the kid's head, running his fingers through Babitch's hair.

"Yes, it is, Murray."

In one swift motion Rucker plunged Babitch's head into the suburban blue swimming pool. Lagonda held his flailing arms as Babitch thrashed wildly about. The kid was groping wildly for the gun in his pants. And then he found it . . .

Joey Randone, having just finished his tour, pulled his car into the Donlan driveway. He heard the shot from the backyard. Joey ran around the side of the house—only cops ran into the sounds of gunfire—and came on the incredible scene at the pool. Babitch was still in the water, smoking gun in his hand. He was choking and screaming. He fired the pistol, again and again. Rucker and Lagonda recoiled from the shots. Amazingly, neither man was armed.

"JESUS, YOU BASTARDS! FUCK YOU," Babitch screamed. Then he ran into the woods.

Joey Randone watched, horrified. It didn't make sense.

"What the fuck are you doing?" Joey asked.

Rucker found his gun and ran after Babitch. Lagonda followed. Ray started to move off, too, but Joey Randone held his sleeve.

"What the fuck, Ray?" Joey said. "You said Lassaro was going to set him up with a new life."

"You think I am that capable, Joey?" Donlan asked. "No, you do not. Or you would not be milk-manning my wife."

Donlan moved off. Randone stood in the backyard, devastated by the truth. He looked up to the Donlans's window in time to see Rose shut off the light.

Rucker and Lagonda were quickly out of breath. Superboy was in twice their shape and running with six times their fury. Donlan finally ran up behind them, puffing harder still. The kid was gone. They were defeated, at least momentarily.

TWENTY-THREE

There was a bit of a breeze in the morning. It would fade by noon. It blew along a line of cars parked on the side, catching pink tickets on their windshields. Jack Rucker came out of the deli on Main Street with a container of coffee. He discovered a ticket under the wiper blade of his car. He looked, at first curious, then astounded. Rage filled him again.

Cindy approached. She studied the tickets, equally curious. Donlan also walked into the picture, holding his coffee.

"What the hell is this?" Rucker asked, waving the ticket.

Cindy shrugged and pointed to a NO PARKING sign above them.

"That is a parking ticket. It's after seven, buddy."

"And what?" Rucker said. "It's after seven—and what?"

"Talk to Freddy," Cindy said. "He wrote it."

Rucker yelled after the deputy as she walked away. Donlan watched them both, his eyes an indictment of the ticket writer.

"You tell 'Wyatt Earp,' that leg of lamb between his ears—that's for *eating,* not thinking, with."

He waved the ticket at Cindy.

"This ticket says this is a green car. Does this car look green to you? It is *blue. Carillon blue.* Tell him I don't own a green car—so I ain't paying no fucking fruitcake ticket."

This wasn't about tickets. Ray Donlan realized that much immediately. He grabbed Rucker by the collar of his shirt and led him off the street as other cops, some off duty and others uniformed on the way in to work, watched.

"You pressed yesterday, Jackie," Donlan said. "You pressed and the guy went up into his attic and found his spine."

Rucker squirmed as Ray continued, whispering. "Now you *chill*. You *chill* and you find my nephew."

Ray walked to his own car then, and smiled back at Rucker, his friend with the Doberman personality.

"Think *Ghandi*," Ray said.

Figs had to give up his room. He wasn't going to share the holding cell in the sheriff's office with real prisoners, even kids arrested on a bullshit collar. Being a cop was still fighting the war between us and them. And no matter how pissed off he got at Ray Donlan and Rucker, Figs was still with the us team. He carried a badge to prove it. And the kids in the cell? Figs couldn't give a shit about them. They were *them*.

So on the day after being arrested for driving through town and thoroughly disturbing a softball game between us and us, the two black teenagers sat in the converted tire storage area. They were beginning to think that by the time this case got to court, they would actually own the town. It was that outrageous, and they knew it.

"This is total racial bullshit, man," one kid said.

Freddy ignored him. He was thumbing through the *New York Post*, which reported that the police and the mayor's office were meeting in a "Big Blue Powwow." Freddy sensed that this, too, was bad news for his town, Cop Land.

"I'm telling you, Freddy, I'm doing you a favor. Just toss 'em."

Figs was sitting on the edge of the dispatcher's desk, sipping coffee. His brain was hemorrhaging, his hangover felt that brutal. Figs was still gray-looking and foul-smelling. He sorted through the In basket on Cindy's desk.

"Figs," she said. "You can't touch that stuff."

Figs was smoking too much, already. He was also fixing his files. Mostly this meant crumpling up pieces of paper and tossing them in a large wastepaper basket he had marked "Out."

"Sheriff!" Cindy said.

Freddy looked up from the fabulous doings on page six.

"Do what Figs says, Cindy," Freddy ordered.

Figs grinned at *his* new deputy. Cindy looked as if she were ready to contribute vomit into the Out basket.

"Yo, yo," one of the kids yelled from behind the bars. He wanted to bum a cigarette. Freddy threw the kid a pack as Figs clapped his hands. After a minute, he got up, unlocked the door, and let the kids walk out of his station.

"Straight home, now," Figs said.

TWENTY-FOUR

Later that night, Freddy stood in the urinal, pondering his life as he emptied his bladder.

By the usual standards, the Four Aces Tavern was deserted. Suddenly Rucker was beside him. Freddy noticed and then flushed the toilet. If only his problems would flush away so neatly. Rucker glared into the light. Even this early, the psychotic cop was in lastcall form.

" 'Stead of writing bullshit tickets, Freddy—which I have no intention of paying—maybe you should be looking into that fire. Ya know, with scrutiny. I mean, my girl at Chase Bank says Figs was missing payments, with that and his co-co problems, why not?"

Freddy turned the whole conversation around. "Where were you that night, Jack?"

Rucker's face went blank. He zipped his pants, but not his mouth.

"Had nothing to do with it. That would be retribution—and that I leave to God almighty. I am *Ghandi*."

Rucker patted water on his face. As the sheriff watched Rucker, he was surprised by two things. Number one was the idea that Figs had burned down his own home. Number two was that Rucker was perfectly willing to rat out another cop. Freddy Heflin, crime dog, was on the case now.

"Figs is the one getting the fat insurance check," Rucker continued.

Freddy was on to new business. He spun on his boot and moved to the door, saying, "Say hello to Superboy when you see him."

Now, Rucker spun. Freddy was still growing his set of *cojones*, as he often heard cops say. Rucker was nervous.

"Superboy is dead, Freddy. We put him in the ground."

Freddy left the bar.

Later Freddy walked into the Four Aces and spotted Ray Donlan and the others sitting at a back table. They were quiet, even tense, as Freddy passed them. Donlan felt he was losing control.

"Freddy," he yelled. "Pull up a chair."

Cindy was sitting at another table. She was on Freddy with the question even before he was seated.

"So where is he?"

"Hmm?"

"*Where is he?*" she repeated.

Upon hearing this question, the bar fell silent. The bar actually seemed to lurch to a stop, like one of the subway cars these cops no longer had to ride to work.

"You know, *Figs,*" Cindy said.

"Oh, yeah," Freddy said. "He's at my house."

The place sighed at the answer. The cops went back to their bad habits.

"Is he just gonna hang around your place now?" Cindy wanted to know.

"I don't know. Is that a problem?"

"I mean—I know he's got plenty of useful tips and all. But when he's around—you know, I feel like a secretary with a gun."

Freddy exhaled deeply. He wouldn't admit it, but some-

times these cops made him feel like that, too. Cindy took a
cigarette from Freddy's pack. Cindy's smoke was interrupted by a scream from another part of the room. They
looked to the sound and saw Joey Randone jump to his feet.
"Help find him? So what can happen? So you can finish
cleaning your pool with his head? When you got something
to tell me, Ray, *Mr. Humanitarian,* you tell me."

Donlan said nothing. He just glared at the man who was
screwing his wife and now refusing to help him fix a police
union matter. Somewhere in the back of Donlan's head a
switch was snapped off. Joey put up his hands in surrender.

"I'm going. I'm in at ten," he announced.

"We all are," Rucker said. "We got another hour to look."

Donlan continued staring. Joey grabbed his coat, avoid-
ing the boss's eyes, and walked out. Rucker studied Donlan
for a message. He was getting tired of the Ghandi thing.

Like the worst of the gangsters, Ray was erasing his
problems one at a time. He turned to check on Freddy again
as Cindy leaned over. She was careful to whisper into her
boss's good ear. "I never should have taken this job," she
said. "You were sweet back then. With your sad music and
your ear. I told my mom you were like this noble turtle. I
thought I had found someone moving at my own speed." She
laughed, lightly. There was more hare in her then Cindy
could ever have imagined.

"But now—I mean—what am I, a doorknob hole? And, I
mean, what are you doing? At least these guys know who
they are. At least they're not staring at old newspaper clippings. What, are you going to like me more if I put on a
fucking tiara and jump off a bridge? Is that gonna make you
feel better?"

Cindy grabbed the check and walked to the coatrack.

*   *   *

Well, they were both bachelors now. Monica was extremely gone. Liz never was, and Cindy never would be. They drank as hard and as deeply as their defeat would allow. By midnight, Freddy and Figs were up to their elbows in empty bottles and chicken bones. They could fill Kentucky Fried Chicken buckets with the bones and empties. They were a drunken, greasy mess.

And still the albums spun on the turntable. Springsteen was playing as Freddy and Figs sat across from each other at the sheriff's empty kitchen table. There was a half-empty bottle of scotch separating their completely vacuous lives. There was a collection of articles on the table centering on the equally blank suicide of Murray Babitch.

"You're lucky your ear kept you off the force, Freddy. It's a deep, dark motherfuck."

"Yeah, whatever, Figs. But I'd like to have discovered that myself, you know?"

"Well," Figs said. "What you're feeling right now— friendless, angry, nervous, misunderstood—that is it. This is the life. City cops ain't nothing but garbagemen. Pick up the trash, take it away, dump it. Next week the same thing. Go down the same block. Pick up the same trash all over again."

Freddy sucked his cigarette down to the filter. He stared out the window, tears welling in his eyes. He would never be capable of doing the one great thing again. He would not matter. He did not have the strength of Figs.

"If I saw Liz—drowning in the water—if I saw that today, I wouldn't go in. I'd stand there—and *I'd think about it*. And that's the best thing I ever did with my life."

Freddy crushed his cigarette out. If only the memory could be snuffed out so easily. "Now I hear all these voices. Telling me I can't do anything."

"What did you hear when you saved her, Freddy?"

His friend smirked and then shrugged. It was a question Figs had always wanted to ask.

"Music," Freddy answered.

Figs smiled. He studied a newspaper picture of Babitch. For the first time he saw the newspaper articles as sheet music waiting to be played. He was excited with the idea.

"So."

"So," Freddy agreed.

"So you want to sit around listening to Gergen Gingle-shirts for the rest of your—"

"Glenn Gould," Freddy corrected him.

"Playing the opus to cunt-hair number six in G flat major labia."

Freddy laughed, then shook his head.

"Or do you want to bring the faggot in, Sheriff? Let him spill."

"I wouldn't know where to begin."

"You ever see *Murder on the Orient Express?*"

Freddy shook his head. Figs smiled, his eyes as bright as the fire that had destroyed his house.

"They all did it."

TWENTY-FIVE

Cops get hurt every night in New York City. They get shot, stabbed, sliced and diced. Every response is a chance to die. But even though they all know dying is a possibility, no one cop ever thinks it is going to happen to him. This cop believed it was happening. His voice on the radio told everyone who listened to it that he could taste death. But now, he just lay on a Bronx roof, smelling of piss and dog shit. He felt something warm and he knew it was his own blood, pooling. He whispered desperately in the darkness over the radio.

"Ah, Christ," the cop exclaimed, wincing against the pain. "Where are you guys? Shit. I'm down, and Joey's trying to hold on. But this bastard, he cut me up. He's a fucking monster."

The cop lay on a tar-paper roof. His neck and thigh were punctured. He struggled to hear the radio.

"We are on the way, Tony. We got a bus coming, too. Hold it together."

"I can't move. I think he cut my tendon."

"Stay put. We are *moving*, Tony."

"I need some assistance over here," Joey yelled across the top of the roof.

"Joey. Where's Joey?" the cop on the radio wanted to know.

"Fifty feet—ah—he's in trouble, Jackie. Responding units be made aware . . ."

There he was. Joey Randone was on the roof of the next building. Well, sort of. A huge black man, Shondel, was holding the cop in the air. The bad guy still had the huge prison muscles. From the look of him he had been home for about ten minutes after doing twenty years in the Attica weight room. Although the guy wore sweats, he did not need them right now. The big man held the cop effortlessly over the side of the building. Shondel brought the cop to his nose and snorted.

"You release me now, you cocksucker."

Shondel laughed at the cop's temper. He was just a little boy in blue.

"You got a wife?" the weightlifter asked.

Joey nodded. He looked about, wildly. There had to be a way out of this. His gun was lying on the roof, empty. Across the street people were watching from their windows. Some gasped at the sight of the uniformed cop being held over the edge. Someone yelled, "Go ahead, drop the motherfucker. He would drop you, black man." Then the spectator slammed his window. This was as bad as New York City got. After a cop was acquitted of choking a kid from this precinct to death last year, a sniper dropped the commander with a rifle shot as he walked to the parking lot to drive home. The Bronx was Fort Apache no more.

"You got a little baby?" Shondel continued.

Again Joey Randone nodded.

"So quit," the guy said. "Just tell me you quit and hate cops. Then you can go home. You can kiss you wife. Eat your baby's Fruit Loops. And it be tasting so good. Just quit, and thank me for letting you live."

Joey blinked but said nothing.

"I can kill you with my hands, I can kill you with your

gun. I can kill you with my blood, too. That's right. I got the virus, too. Or I can let you go. You would still be a hero to me. 'Cause I be re-demed. Rer-re-re-redeemed."

A siren sounded. It meant nothing to this maniac. As lights swirled down the block, he tightened his grip. Joey began to cry. He wiped his mouth on his shoulder. He realized then that he was going to die.

Freddy sat on his porch, fascinated with a Figs police narration. He studied Figs as he purposely tipped a can over and beer leaked out.

"Say you got a brother cop in deep shit—he is down and he's bleeding. And you gotta get there—but there's no green lights. All over the city, you got red lights."

"You go through the red lights," Freddy said, trying to solve the riddle. Figs was disappointed with the response.

"Sure, Freddy, you fire up the roof, you wail, you go through the red lights. But it is slow fighting your way through traffic. And *they* can hear you coming. The goal is perpetual motion. You want greens, but how do you insure greens? You can't. As in life, as in traffic. So you leave yourself an out. At every corner, you leave yourself an alternative. Follow?"

Freddy shrugged. He could not even tail Figs through a conversation, how was he going to chase him through the streets of New York? He moved his hands in a zigzag course, approaching the tipped bottle on the railing. Maybe Freddy did understand.

"You move diagonal," Figs said. "You turn the wheel when you hit a red light. You don't drive down Broadway to get to *Broadway*. Life is about navigation, Freddy. *Motion advancement toward your goal.*"

Figs righted the tipped beer can and smiled.

"You move diagonal, you get perpetual motion."

"But," Freddy asked, "how does this apply to us here, in Garrison?"

Figs spun around, impatient with Freddy's deafness.

"It applies, Freddy! Jesus. It's just as easy to tail a man walking in front of you. You butt heads with these buddies of ours. *You come at them head on?* With pink, freaking, parking tickets?"

Freddy shook his head and rested against the railing. He looked out over Garrison.

"They got lives, Freddy, families. They come from someplace. They have a trail. You know where they are, and where they are going."

Figs spoke in a low voice so Freddy had to lean in to hear him. "You move diagonal. You jag. It may feel innately wrong. But like so much in this world, what feels innately wrong is innately right."

The street was a raging red strobe light. The cops were panning the roof as the squad cars arrived, screeching; helicopters were searching for the monster and the cop. As the cars pulled up, the cops jumped out, guns drawn, and sprinted for the ten-story brick tenement building. One of the last cars to arrive belonged to Lieutenant Ray Donlan. He was being chauffeured by Jack Rucker. Donlan moved more slowly than the others. Maybe this was because he was in charge.

The cops ran around in circles, searching some of the neighbors who were pointing to the sky and the tar-paper roofs. Cops banged on steel reinforced doors, trying to get into the abandoned building and up the stairs to the injured cops. One cop tried to crawl down a decaying fire escape. Down the alley, Ray Donlan came on an open door. It led to a stairwell that spiraled upward. Donlan pushed the door shut again—silently—before Rucker and another cop arrived.

"It's locked," he lied.

There was an anguished scream from above. They all recognized Joey's voice.

"Joey's in trouble, Ray."

Donlan nodded and pulled a locksmith's pick from his pocket. He jiggled a pin to open the door as they watched. The cops waited impatiently as Donlan mimed picking the lock. They did not think to try to open the unlocked door. Another hideous scream came from above them.

"One second," Donlan said.

"Let's break it down," one cop screamed.

"No need," Ray said. "I got it—just one more."

Ten seconds later, Donlan pulled open an unlocked door. The cops raced past him and up the stairwell.

Above them, Shondel and Randone were wrestling for control. The cop lost the battle as soon as the monster grabbed him. Now the guy slashed his knife across Randone's hands. He threw him over. Randone grabbed a television antenna and held on. As the cops ran up the stairs, they could hear him screaming. He was losing his grip. By the time the cops hit the landing, he was gone. Donlan still hadn't reached the landing, but the rest of the cops were there, looking over the side. Joey Randone hit the sidewalk with a muffled *thunk.*

Still, from above, there was a finality to the sound. Ray Donlan—police boss and secret cop killer—stepped on to the roof as Joey hit. He saw all of the men staring down, looking silent and shocked. Rucker turned and glared at Donlan, who winced but then looked off. The mistake was getting cleaner all the time. He couldn't wait to break the news to his wife.

* * *

At this same early morning hour, across the river, Freddy lay awake in bed. The television droned on, just noise. Figs was still knocking around the house somewhere, and Freddy could hear running water. He was thinking about Liz again, and wondering if she would ever come back to him. He had mistreated Cindy, who was only decent, capable, and attractive. He didn't deserve either of them. He wondered what Liz was wearing right now and how alone she was.

Still, his eyes were open and bloodshot. Figs wasn't a bad roommate, he thought, once you got past his binge drinking and speeches. He didn't mind cleaning up, and he answered the phone. He was smarter than Freddy, sure. But the sheriff was not intimidated by intelligence. He thought of Liz again. The longing for her was constant and ruinous. Love must be a chronic toothache, Freddy decided.

There was a knock at his front door again. Hopeful, Freddy sat up. He checked his hair in the mirror and wondered how he would explain her to Figs.

Freddy walked to the door and opened it onto a wild, unshaven man. Where Freddy had expected to find Liz, Murray Babitch had found him.

"You're the sheriff, right?"

Freddy stepped back and blinked in bewilderment. He nodded and touched his nose. Babitch spoke in a paranoid whisper. His eyes were searching and yet trusting. He was like any cop called to respond to a domestic dispute. Only he was the tragedy waiting to happen. His words staggered out.

"Hey," Murray Babitch said. "I'm the cop who jumped. The one they buried. *I'm dead.* I mean, I need your help. They're trying to kill me."

"Who?" Freddy asked.

"*Who?*" Babitch said. He laughed, then wept. "Are you alive? Who? Do you live here?"

Freddy wiped his face with his hand. He didn't even know why he'd asked the question. He did not mean to be so naive, so uncoplike.

"Okay. So. Uh. What do you want to do? You want to go to the city?"

"Go to the city?! Jesus. Do you have any idea how connected he is? *Do you? Go to the city? This guy is fucking everywhere.*"

Figs walked out of the bathroom, a towel to his face. Babitch saw him first, and he was terrified. He saw Figs as one of *them* in his tale. He was thoroughly confused. For Murray Babitch, there was no us anymore. Figs and Freddy met eyes. The sheriff turned back to Babitch, but he bounded away from them like a deer from an accident.

Rounding a bend along the Garrison meadowlands, they bounced and chugged, Freddy wearing his bathrobe. Figs was farther back. Babitch was far ahead. He was a fast, dangerous man. It was uncanny how the guy made himself invisible. Having lost him, Freddy slowed. He could imagine then, how it had happened on the bridge. The cop was a wiry, crazed man. And when the lights were turned on, and he needed to escape, Murray Babitch had the dexterity of a thin cockroach. He was all flailing arms and legs until he disappeared behind a wall.

"Shit," Freddy said.

The sheriff turned, and faced an approaching car. He studied the lights until he realized it was nobody. It was just a funkified VW van filled with suburban slackers. Smoke billowed out as the van passed.

Suddenly, Figs joined him, coughing. They looked around, but saw nothing but reeds. In that light, the water tower, the emptiest reed of them all, looked huge over Garrison.

Freddy slept with the gun next to him that night. He stared at the blinking red clock until morning. Figs slept on the couch.

At dawn, Freddy stood at the sink and splashed water over his face. Freddy looked at himself in the mirror and wondered how cops felt looking at themselves in the mirror. Then he noticed a sprinkling of white powder on a hand mirror. He ran his finger through the powder and sniffed at it.

"You waking up?" Figs said from behind him. "I feel like shit."

Figs sniffled. "Fucking allergies," he lied.

Freddy was filled with dread then, but it was a knowing dread. And the knowing was empowering.

TWENTY-SIX

$\mathbf{A}$ couple of days later, they held another police funeral in town. This one wasn't as big as the ceremony for Murray Babitch. And that was strange. The cop on the bridge was a suicide. He had also shot a couple of innocent people to death in a drunken moment. Randone was killed, murdered after encountering a crazed monster on parole. The second death said more about everyday police encounters, but it didn't have the same legs in the paper.

Still, they came again. The blue sea rolled over the town. The bagpipers blew a desperate wail over the hill again. The helicopters flew their flawed formation and the politicians came again to stand with the mourning cops.

The television moths flocked to the same lights on the same hill. This time they had a widow and young child to focus on. So what they missed in storyline, they made up for in mournful pictures.

Liz Randone was lovely, and strangely numb. They came for her in the middle of the night, as they always did. She heard the knock at the door, and came down. As soon as she saw the chaplain at the door, she knew Joey had been shot.

"How bad?" she asked.

"The worst," the police chaplain replied. He reached to catch her but Liz did not fall. Her reaction was telling. The chaplain had been through this enough to know the couple had had problems.

Rucker was with them. He was there by department design, too. He did not tell the story kindly. But he did put more of a pace in Lieutenant Donlan's movement than had existed on the steps. He lied and said that most guys, when they knew they were going to hit the pavement, died before they ever hit the ground.

"Their hearts just burst, Mrs. Randone," the chaplain lied.

Every policeman's wife knew the dreaded routine. They had talked about it as they measured out their lives over coffee and beer. They discussed "getting the knock": at over a hundred barbecues, birthdays, christenings, and graduations. *The knock at the door.* They all dreaded it. She went with them immediately, kissing the baby on the cheek before she left. They had brought a baby-sitter with them.

They flew by helicopter to the hospital. The mayor met her in person on the hospital floor.

"I am so sorry," he said. "The city thanks you."

This one was the Florence Nightingale of mayors. Liz used to joke that he showed up every time a cop suffered a bruise. But the mayor who loved cops never gave them a raise. He preferred to pay them in useless tears. He cried at their funerals and they cried at his press conferences.

Still, knowing all this, Liz Randone did not push the politician away. She was glad to have the hug, even a false one, that night. She saw the television lights and the reporters. She knew their role in this loss, too, and at first she was not angry. Only on the second day did she begin to see them as intruders. By the morning of the funeral, she saw them as vultures.

Liz was not big on self-pity. There were younger widows in the NYPD, she knew, and women who certainly hated their husbands more than Liz did. Once, when the police chaplain knocked to break the bad news, a woman put a bullet through the door. She was expecting her husband.

Loss gave meaning to the failed lives and marriages of many widows. Police Officer John Doe wasn't a drunken, cheating piece of shit after all. He was a dead hero. The cop could be recalled and re-created by a widow in stages, most of them happier. Memory was kind that way. One, a nineteen-year-old from Wayne, married a week after her high school graduation, was called The Baby Widow.

Liz knew that she would not be able to survive the death of her husband in the same house they had shared. There were a lot of things that bothered her, one of the worst being the smell of her husband's jackets, still hanging in his closet. The smell would fade with the memory, she knew. But it was so unfair. She wanted it to end differently. And then, on the morning of the funeral, she walked into the bathroom and saw his toothbrush in the glass. And that was what Liz Randone saw as she studied the casket at Joey's grand funeral: his toothbrush in the glass.

Liz made a graceful widow, the wives all agreed. Rose Donlan had the sense not to come. Liz stood against the pain, resolute and lovely. Her hair blew in the wind. Her grasp of the child's hand was firm. The baby laughed at one point and the crowd shuddered as Liz allowed the child to wear her father's hat.

Freddy watched with obsessive interest. Liz did not waver as the cops and friends from town formed another receiving line for another cop.

Liz discovered Freddy's eyes on her and looked back, easily. She still found comfort in Freddy's eyes. The sentences offered to Liz were but a version of the ones offered the mother of Murray Babitch under this same tent, in the same spot, a few days ago.

"He was a great guy, Liz."
"We are all your family now."
"Just call if you need anything."

Ray Donlan passed through the line, but did not have words. He just smiled grimly. It was strange being in the cemetery for the lieutenant. There were too many cops here. Too many friends. He smiled as he walked off, careful to avoid Glenn Tunney's headstone. Ray Donlan was in a hurry. He was moving much faster now than he had moved for Joey Randone. The lieutenant had work to do. Ray Donlan, the cornered man, was looking to fill the Garrison cemetery further still.

"Find my nephew," he said to Rucker on the way out.

TWENTY-SEVEN

Freddy emerged from the PATH train station early the next morning. The twin towers still amazed him, and he stared up into the glass like any other tourist. He kept walking until he stood in the great arch of the Manhattan Municipal Building. Chambers Street was behind him. It ran directly to the Hudson. Jersey was as long a fly ball away as Darryl Strawberry hit them for the Mets and the Yankees. Across the way rose One Police Plaza, the oddly colored building the cops in the Four Aces Tavern liked to call "The Purple Palace." Several cops stood with protestors outside a blue barricade of sawhorses. One cop watched Freddy intently. Their eyes met, and Freddy recognized Berta Combs from the bomb squad. They had met in the Four Aces Tavern just a few weeks ago. Freddy had quit pinball since then. He nodded to her and recalled her exchange with his friend Figs.

Freddy showed his identification at the door and was escorted up to the secret offices in the back elevator. No one rode with him but the silent, steady escort. Once you got swallowed this deep in the big rat's intestines, cops said, names were on a need-to-know basis. And no one needed to know Freddy's name after he walked through the metal

detector at the front desk of One Police Plaza. He showed
the security guards Moe Tilden's card at the front desk.

"Please, be discreet," Freddy said.

But that was all the cops knew. By the time Freddy arrived on the thirteenth floor the war room was subdued. The
detectives spoke in a whisper while looking back toward
Moe Tilden.

Lieutenant Moe Tilden was visible through a doorway.
He sat, a cigarette burning in his lips, his feet on his desk.
He looked glum, and strangely disconnected. He played
with a rubber band.

"What's up?" a cop asked, unwrapping his lunch. "What
the fuck happened to us?"

Another detective spoke lowly as he swallowed a potato
chip. "The PDA went to the powerhouse. The powerhouse
went to the mayor's office, who called the first dep, who
called the chief of inspections. They pulled the plug. They
told Moe if he sets foot in Jersey again, he's back in the bag."

Carson timidly approached Tilden's door. Moe did not
see him coming. He was dreaming about catching bluefish
again. Specifically, Moe was thinking back to his first corrupt cop, Henry Wadsworth. He was a thief and a crack-
head, Moe remembered, but an absolute degenerate
fisherman. Uncle Moe liked to fish, too. The first thing Moe
watched Henry buy with stolen drug money was a sixteen-
foot Boston Whaler with twin Mercury engines. Henry was
a scummer and a skimmer. Moe watched the boat in the
water a week later.

No, Moe did not see Carson. He didn't see much when
his wheels were spinning. The same thing happened every
time they pulled the plug on him. Tilden always went back
to the first guy, and bluefish, as he tried to remember why
he fished so intensely for corrupt cops. The memory always

put the Internal Affairs boss back in the mood to catch some blues.

Out in Jamaica Bay and Long Island Sound the fish were just beginning their summer spawning run. By early summer the waters would be bubbling with frenzied schools of bluefish. They hunted in hunting parties half a mile wide and an eighth of a mile long.

They were a strong, pugnacious breed—a fish that could weigh as much as thirty pounds and fight twice its weight. They were built like missiles with long, sharp, and irregular teeth. They had delicate blue scales and a thin backbone. Fishermen like Henry Wadsworth considered them a demented fish—hunters that lost all self-control in the presence of too much of a good thing.

When the blues were running, a school of them would slam into a fisherman's boat, slopping against the side and devouring anything he threw into his bait slick—chopped-up mackerel, butterfish, cigarette butts, paper, even beer cans. Excited bluefish would eat, vomit, and eat again. They thought nothing of taking single bites out of fish in their own feeding pack. And if a fisherman kept a blue on the line too long, a larger one might come along and swallow it. Once you got a school of blues into a frenzy, it was impossible not to catch them.

The blues were Moe Tilden's favorite fish, too. He liked the fight in them and the fact that though they always traveled in great blue waves, they only cared about preserving themselves. The fish were not unlike the fish Henry Wadsworth swam with in Brooklyn. The blue-jacketed cops stole everything they saw once they got into a feeding frenzy. Everything from radios and televisions to car parts and garbage cans. Drugs and cash were impossible for these bluefish not to steal. Henry was an odd man. Moe had watched him sitting on a boat purchased with stolen drug

money and reeling in a fish. Henry always measured his
fish. If one was too small, he threw it back. Moe wondered
what kind of person would steal so much and yet follow another set of rules on the water. When Uncle Moe finally
caught Henry, and got him to turn, he made a very simple
plea. "Let's go catch some blues," Moe had suggested. And
then had promised to let the cop keep his boat. The guy
agreed to help because he liked the sport of it. Now Carson
was standing before Moe Tilden, demanding attention.

"Moe," Carson said. He said the name three times before
Tilden answered.

"Uh, yeah."

"The sheriff of Garrison, New Jersey, is here to see you."

Tilden's face was surprised, even numb. He hadn't expected to find a bit of fisherman in Freddy Heflin.

"Y' gonna tell him we're frozen?" Carson asked.

Tilden was thinking. And smiling. He stood, picked up a
stack of files, and put them into an empty box. He tossed
another box to Carson, who stood, puzzled.

"Put your files in here," Tilden said.

"What?"

"Throw them in here. Do it. We're done."

"Moe? What the fuck?"

Tilden stepped into the war room and quickly turned
to a detective. "Rubin? What are you doing? This case is
closed."

The detective was scared, and confused. "Uh, yeah. But
you told me to—"

"Forget what I told you. *Fuck you.* This case is closed.
Go to lunch." Tilden threw this cop's work into the trash,
too.

"GO TO LUNCH," he thundered.

"But I got . . ."

* * *

Tilden crossed the room and ripped the map of Garrison from the board and stuffed it into the trash. The stunned cops watched the tantrum, amazed. Tilden moved along the detectives' desks, throwing files to the floor. Everyone in the room was convinced that their boss had suddenly gone mad.

"This case is fucking closed! Get the fuck out of here! All of you."

The detectives shuffled out of the room. Carson looked at his boss, dumbstruck. Tilden grinned and Carson blinked into the man's apparent madness.

"Carson, put your work in the box, too."

He did as ordered, stuffing his work into the box now marked "Operation Cop Land." Tilden stepped over the mess he'd made and back into his office. Freddy got off the elevators and passed three cops on their way out. He passed some more dejected cops in the stairwell.

Freddy stepped into the war room, surprised by the mess. Carson sat at his desk, dumping files.

"Sheriff, what can I do for you?"

Freddy looked about the room, bewildered. He approached the detective. Freddy had expected more of a reception.

"What's going on?" Freddy asked. "You guys moving?"

Carson smiled cryptically. He continued to stuff his boxes full of work.

"You could say that."

Freddy nodded toward Tilden.

"He told me to come down if—you know."

"Uh-huh."

Freddy was confused. He furrowed his brow. "Look. *You guys were right.* Babitch is alive."

In the back office Tilden listened. He was gleeful but remained hidden. He snapped the rubber band as a fisherman snaps back the lead. Freddy was ready to flop across the floor like a big tuna to get attention and prove his worth if he needed to. Nothing works as well as desperation. Instead of diving into bubbles after a car, Freddy was throwing the Internal Affairs cops a life vest. Tilden had guessed, and had created a scene to trap a hero. Freddy had walked right into it.

Freddy tried to get into Tilden's office but Carson stepped in front of him, saying, "It is a little late, Sheriff," Carson said. "But—thanks for coming in anyway." Freddy turned. He was absolutely confused. He nodded toward Tilden, again.

"Sheriff. Look around you. It's out of our hands now. You dig."

"I gotta talk to him. It's important."

Freddy tried to run around Carson. He opened Tilden's door and stepped in. "Hey," Freddy said.

Tilden just sat there. He refused to meet Freddy's eyes. He turned his back on Freddy and looked out the window, lighting a fresh cigarette. Carson entered the room and pulled on Freddy's sleeve.

"Hey, you were right," Freddy began again. "They tried to kill him. Like you said. But he got away. He's running around, crazy, in the woods, you know, like Grizzly Adams or something. He's scared to death. We gotta do something."

"He should be scared," Carson said. "His uncle got this case closed with one phone call."

Freddy shook off Carson's false grip. "Look, I'm sorry—it took so long to come around, you know? You were right. I couldn't see the truth. But like you said, the evidence. My loyalties were confused, you know. But I'm ready."

Tilden was stone-faced, still. He was an expert, patient fisherman.

"What is this? You come to me, to *my* town with these speeches," Freddy said.

"That was two weeks ago," Tilden said. He was still looking out the window.

"What about Babitch?" Freddy said.

"Fuck him."

"What about Donlan?"

"Fuck him."

"What about Joey Randone?"

"He fell off a building."

Freddy glared.

"Listen to me, Sheriff. I'm very sorry I woke you from your slumber. But it's over. My hands are tied now. You shut me down."

"No. It's not done. You can—"

Tilden finally turned and faced Freddy. He was red-faced, intense.

"*Listen to me.* I offered you a chance. *Listen to me, you deaf fuck.* When there was still room to move, I offered you a chance to be a cop. *And you blew it.*"

Freddy spoke slowly, his eyes blazing with emotion. "You know, everyone says that—'Listen to me, Freddy. Listen to me, Sheriff.' You know? I got one good ear. But I listen hard to the words."

Tilden munched a sandwich, seemingly oblivious to Freddy. He cursed the sandwich maker.

"But what comes out of everyone's mouth is bullshit."

"Hear this, you deaf fuck . . . *You blew it.*"

"I've heard things about you, too, Moe Tilden."

"Oh yeah?"

"You're no better than them. This isn't about the law. *You people are all the same.*"

Tilden was silent. Carson looked to some detectives assembled at the door. Freddy walked off, past them. Carson turned to Tilden as he left. Smoke trickled out of the secret watcher's lips.

"That cupcake makes a mess. We have a case again."

"Do you think he can do it?"

"Sheriff Freddy Heflin is capable of great things," Moe Tilden said.

TWENTY-EIGHT

One of the great social rivalries in the city was the Battle of Badges, the bitter war being waged between the cops and the firemen, New York's City's Finest against its Bravest. The civil-service war pitted brother against brother, father against son, and even mother against daughter. There was even one case of a female police officer who gave birth to a son who grew up to become, alas, a fireman. Upon his graduation, she gave the boy a pair of fire engine–red leotards. Mama Cop viewed fire fighting as sissy work. The rivalry was that biting.

The hockey games between the Bravest and the Finest were legendary, legendary brawls. The fights on the ice were mirrored by the fights in the stands. One year the two teams played to a nothing-nothing tie. The two teams punched each other up and down the ice until only the goalies were left standing. There was so much crap thrown on the ice—fire hoses, handcuffs, and fake badges—that the games regularly had to be suspended after two periods.

"Game misconduct on the crowd," the mayor announced. He couldn't decide which side to sit on.

Each department also had a boxing team and a football team. The fights became so bad during the boxing matches at the Felt Forum that they held the match a couple of times with no spectators allowed in the stands. It was a battle of

Irish civil service. Sisters married to cops and firemen didn't speak to each other for years and years. One woman divorced a well-known cop and then married a fireman just to piss the guy off.

"I'm getting the real *hose* now," she would tell his friends.

It was insanity and it was metropolitan New York. And God forbid that the cops arrest a fireman for drunk driving. They fought each other to save lives at accident scenes, too, before the mayor intervened. Hero work was provided on a first come, first save basis. Cops were called to one scene when firemen attached the Jaws of Life to a patrol car after the cops had refused to let the fireman pull a trapped man out of an auto.

Still, they were brothers. They attended the same wakes, weddings, and christenings. When someone robbed a fireman, the cops gave the guy an extra little beating. And when the fireman came upon a burning house that belonged to a cop, they gave the fire an extra little stomping.

But they never would have attended the same July Fourth barbecue. They didn't even do that in Breezy Point, a closed community of cops and firemen near the Rockaways. There was even a gate on the way into that community.

There was still another community of cops and firemen called Broad Channel. This wooden neighborhood was built on a narrow strip of highway between Howard Beach and Far Rockaway. It was the last neighborhood in the city to get electricity and phone service. It was the city outback, and the first gathering point for cops and firemen. It was a rough spot, still, a white pocket like a little Appalachia. A few years before, when some neighborhood kids had gone downstairs and discovered a black token booth clerk on the A train stop, they had firebombed the booth. They were doing life now, but they were both on the police hiring list when they killed the guy.

Broad Channel was a white ghetto only two blocks deep on either side. It was all shacks now, a trailer park of white trash. Breezy Point, on the other hand, was a classy collecting point throughout the fifties, sixties, and seventies. It was the original Garrison, the first Cop Land, as Moe Tilden would say. Then white flight happened. Blacks and Jews were still unwelcome in Breezy Point, but the place was surrounded by *them,* as the cops said. Steadily, the cop island that was Breezy Point just ran out of lawn.

Once they'd called this place the Irish Riviera, but now the overbuilt place—a one-bar town, no less—was just a white, barefoot, summer ghetto. Young cops now summered in Westhampton and South Jersey. City cops still had the same old togetherness, but now the highways and trains were better and they lived in the suburbs.

So the Garrison Fire House barbecue, a gathering of cops and firemen, would have been a social impossibility in the city. But in Garrison, where many of the cops served as volunteer firemen, there was usually no trouble. The gathering was a delightful celebration. Carnival trucks filled an athletic field. The infield was alive with games of chance. There were elephants that spun at each other, little railroad cars for the kids, and a spidery Tilt-A-Whirl. Cop families roamed about. Some cop kids even carried fire trucks. There was no hatred between cops and firemen in Garrison, no caste system between heroes. But then again, there were only a few people of color around.

The cops gathered around a grill where Ray Donlan turned quartered chickens. He looked haggard as he watched Freddy walk through the carnival grounds. As he walked along some people shouted hello at Freddy. Most people just glared at him. They were at war now. And it was odd to watch the sheriff walking through his town fair. Freddy, stone-faced and silent, did not look much different than the sheriff Gary Cooper had played as he walked through the gauntlet his town had become in *High Noon*. Like that sheriff, Freddy was a hated man. A carnival for kids was as dangerous as any alley these same cops patrolled in Harlem and Bedford-Stuyvesant.

Freddy came upon a BB gun–shooting gallery around the open end of a truck. The operator was unshaven and as green as the stuffed turtles that hung above his head. Freddy wanted a turtle for a couple of reasons. The Randone kid liked turtles. That would please Liz. And Cindy had called him a turtle. So the turtle worked for Freddy on a couple of fronts.

He put down two dollars and picked up a gun.

"Two shots in the center," Freddy said.

"Oh, no," the operator said. "You're a cop. Rules are different for cops. I'm losing my shirt here."

"What do I gotta do?"

"Five out of six."

Jack Rucker was suddenly behind Freddy, a full plate in his hands. He picked up a pistol. The operator sighed. He had already decided to skip bringing his show to this cop town next year. The whole freaking town was an arcade game.

"I know, I heard you," Rucker said.

He was wearing sunglasses. He aimed left-handed over a pair of sunglasses. Freddy aimed his gun, too. Maybe this was juvenile, but the competition sure seemed deadly to the sheriff.

"Enjoy your trip to the big city, Freddy?"

Bang! Freddy flinched, and missed. *Bang!* Rucker put his shot in the center.

"Have to make the next five to win now, Freddy."

Freddy turned back to the target, and raised his gun to his eye. All sound seemed to evaporate as he squinted at the target.

Bang! Center. *Bang!* Center. *Bang!* Center. *Bang!* Center. *Bang!* Bull's-eye.

The operator took a drag on his cigarette. He reluctantly handed Freddy a turtle. It was the same turtle Joey Randone had won for his daughter on these same grounds last year. Rucker sneered, though impressed.

As Freddy walked away, Rucker quickly snapped off four shots of his own. He handed the operator the gun back with one BB left in it.

"Always save one round for yourself," Rucker said. "And *keep* the fucking turtle."

TWENTY-NINE

Cindy saw the sheriff coming, and felt a flush. Cindy was leaning on the side of the sheriff's office, chatting up a passerby. The sheriff was carrying foil-wrapped chicken, flowers, and the turtle.

"Well, now, would you look at him," Cindy said almost to herself. She assumed the gifts were for her. But Freddy walked directly past his deputy, averting his eyes.

She was about to ask "Where you going?" but caught herself. She was learning to handle betrayal.

Freddy climbed into his patrol car. He threw the flowers, the turtle, and the food onto the seat beside him. They landed next to a bottle of wine. He wouldn't have been much of a gangster. He never looked in the backseat.

"Hey, where are you going?" Rucker asked from the backseat. Lagonda was sitting next to him. Freddy did not turn around, but checked them in the rearview mirror. He thought then of a garroting scene from *The Godfather*.

Freddy stiffened but tried to be friendly.

"None of your business, guys."

Rucker grabbed Freddy by the hair on the back of his head. "Just 'cause Ray likes you, Freddy, don't mean I'm gonna let you fuck him up the ass," Rucker said.

Freddy winced under Rucker's grip.

"Where is Superboy?" Lagonda asked then.

"You're asking me? I don't know." Freddy slid his right hand toward his gun. Rucker anticipated the movement. From the backseat, there was the metallic, rolling *click* of a revolver.

"You think you're making the big play, Freddy?"

"I'm not making a play, Jack—but—I am the sheriff."

"So who you gonna arrest, Sheriff, the whole town?" Rucker demanded. "Huh? You going to Internal Affairs for paint-by-numbers cop lessons? Are you becoming a cheese eater?

Lagonda picked it up there. Freddy said nothing.

"You think we stink? You think we have an odor? You give jobs to Elmira girls who open their legs. That's not kosher, is it?"

The cops glared through the back of his head.

"Everybody is watching you, Freddy," Rucker said.

And then they just opened the doors, holstered their guns, and got out.

THIRTY

He felt guilty standing on the porch of the dead cop's house. Freddy had been on the Randone porch more in the last two weeks than he'd been in the last two years. He whistled lightly against the nervousness as he knocked on the door again. His arms were full. And so was his heart. It was a lovely late afternoon.

Liz peered at him through a side window. She was surprised, certainly, but brightened at the sight of Sheriff Freddy Heflin.

She opened the door to him.

"Hello."

"Hello, Freddy."

There was a full awkward and dead moment between them. Freddy pushed the flowers into the silence.

"Um, I thought maybe . . . Have you eaten?"

Liz stepped back and Freddy followed her into the kitchen. She was holding his flowers. "Beautiful," she said. "And no *condolences*."

Freddy felt a little caddish and dirty. Embarrassed, he put the plush green turtle on a chair. Liz noticed it and smiled. "Did you win that?"

Freddy nodded proudly. Liz smiled oddly, queasy with memory. "I had to take the other Ollie away from her—he was leaking all over the place."

Liz took the bottle of wine and found a corkscrew. "I haven't been very receptive to visitors."

"Well, if you don't feel like company . . ."

"No, no. Stay. Caroline is napping, and I was sitting in front of the TV wondering if my life is over."

Liz handed Freddy a glass.

"Sounds fun."

Liz opened the tinfoil on the chicken.

"It's probably cold by now," Freddy said.

"I'll heat it up."

Freddy wandered about the living room. He was taking in the room like a prospective customer. He pinched a couch cushion. He had no self-awareness, but certainly meant no offense. He was just wondering what comfort felt like.

"So," Liz said finally. "All that hoopla for Joey. Those ceremonies must give you a headache."

Freddy shrugged off the topic, though he realized that some mourners like to talk through every piece of the funeral, again and again.

"I guess you're getting used to it, huh?" Liz said. "Bury one every two weeks." She crossed into the living room.

"It was like one of the Kennedys died. I thought, Here I am, playing Jackie O."

Freddy was sitting on the couch. He smiled a small, anxious smile. This felt unseemly, but he looked at Liz and easily got through his uneasiness.

"Is this in bad taste? You can tell me, Freddy. It probably is. I'm sorry."

He never saw the Garrison squad car passing the house. It wasn't hard to figure out where Freddy had disappeared to anyway. It didn't take a detective to figure out the passion of Freddy Heflin.

Cindy Betts studied the sheriff's smashed squad car as she rolled slowly past the house. He'd parked the thing in her driveway, Cindy saw. He had no discretion, she decided, or valor.

An Olds Delta 88 slowed as it passed the house. Cindy recognized the driver as Jack Rucker. He smiled at her and followed her gaze to Freddy's car. Cindy's car began to lurch away, but Rucker was quick. He threw his car into reverse and blocked her. He smiled again. There were two other cops in the back of his car.

"Nothing better to do than watch," Rucker said.

"Come on, Jack," a cop yelled from the backseat. "We don't have time for this Romeo and Juliet crap. We gotta get down there. I want to get this done."

Cindy snapped her head away from the conversation. She did not want to hear, see, or talk. She was worse off than Freddy now. Blind, deaf, and mute. By choice.

Rucker grinned at her discomfort.

"We are looking for a lost brother," the sadist cop said. "Be at the Aces later when you get tired of this."

As the sun set inside the neat Randone home, Freddy and Liz sat at the dining room table. They were eating. The television played quietly in the background.

"Figs talks like everyone is a car and you can just, just change directions by turning the wheel. It's not that easy."

"Damn right."

"Sometimes I feel like a boat. A big boat."

"An ocean liner."

"Yeah. The *Queen Mary*."

"The *Titanic*."

"Right," Freddy continued, now inspired. "Exactly. And you see this iceberg coming—you know—but you are so enormous that you can't turn. You have to, like, you know, in the movies, you gotta alert the engine room or the rudder room. And it takes so long you can't turn. You just hit."

Freddy looked up from his fevered story of a slow-motion death, and met Liz's eyes.

"I just hope you're not trying to prove anything, Freddy."

Freddy blinked. He was hurt. Didn't she think he was still capable of great heroic action?

"I mean, okay, some of them are assholes—think they're high priests or something. But why would they go through all this? I mean, maybe they're doing the right thing."

"Liz. I saw pictures of Ray meeting with this guy—this mobster."

"Says who? Internal Affairs?"

"And even you said Joey's death was a—"

"Joey fell off a building, Freddy."

Freddy found the graduation picture of her husband on the wall. He was all blue and polish. He had a ribbon on his chest. A big grin.

"I don't need this, you know, opened up. Maybe you need this, Freddy. But I *don't*. I mean, all Joey wanted for us was a place to live. I mean, who are you to judge till you've walked in their shoes." She paused a beat. "Maybe that's what you're trying to do with me."

The baby, Caroline, began to cry. Liz rose sadly as Freddy stiffened. So there you had the difference between them. Liz would not dive in to save the same man who'd dived in to rescue her. She climbed the stairs.

Freddy sighed and turned to the television, dejected. He hit the Mute switch and turned to a cop movie. Treat Williams was starring in *Prince of the City*. Freddy had long since reached the point in life where memory and history were a television soundtrack. He turned up the volume against his own reality.

"Cops are nothing but garbagemen," the smoking cop actor said. Pick up the trash. Dump it. Next week, you pick up the same trash all over again."

Freddy blinked at the screen. That must be true. He'd heard the same speech this week from a real cop.

THIRTY-ONE

Freddy was driving along the marshland at night. He passed a number of cars by the water. Flashlights scanned the brush. Everyone was searching for Babitch. His deputy, Bill, watched from a squad car parked nearby. Freddy pulled his car up and faced the deputy. He was a little surprised by how much the harmless fellow knew. The secret death and life of Superboy now seemed to belong to the entire town. In order to preserve it, and clean up his situation, Ray Donlan would have to eliminate half the town and build a new cemetery for his work.

Not that, from what Freddy knew, the lieutenant and his mob friends would mind that much.

"Donlan caught his wife dropping food around here," Bill reported. "So they figure he must be nearby."

Freddy nodded, weary with the news and his town.

"You know why they called him Superboy?"

" 'Cause he was a hero," Freddy said.

Bill shook his head. It had nothing to do with the Brooklyn matter. Geisler had learned more about that, too. Some cops were robbing a crack house in Red Hook. Babitch was not in on the shakedown. He wasn't even there at first. On their way out of the place one of the cops knocked over a kerosene lantern by mistake. The crooked cops could barely get off the block before the building ignited. The cops were selling drugs through a mail slot on the second floor. The customer couldn't see through the slot so they had no idea they were buying vials of crack from uniformed cops.

Anyway, Bill learned, Babitch passed the burning building on his way to work. He was in street clothes. A woman was standing on the street crying, "My babies, my babies." She was living illegally and rent-free in the basement. Babitch never thought twice. He just dove right in and pulled the kids out of the fire. *Just saw the bubbles and dove right in.*

Bill pointed to some soup cans by the sheriff's front wheel. "Because he loves Campbell's chicken and stars soup. *Soup*erboy. Get it?" Bill smiled. He liked this story better than the one about saving black babies from a burning building. But Freddy just drove off. Nothing was what it seemed in this town, even the nicknames.

Freddy walked into his house an hour or so later. He turned off his personal alarm system once he got inside and took off his coat. He turned to find an envelope on the kitchen table. It was addressed to Figs from State Farm Insurance. A green check was sticking out. Figs walked into the room then, carrying clean clothes. He folded them and put them into a familiar, though slightly charred, NYPD athletic bag.

"You got your check," Freddy said.

"Thanks to you, Freddy, filling out those papers in such a timely fashion."

Freddy blinked into the lie.

"You with Liz?"

The sheriff nodded. Half the town knew by sunset. Freddy's mind was working on something else. He stared at the slightly charred bag, remembered when he had seen it last. It was in the bar with the woman from the bomb squad.

Freddy weighed the evidence as Figs crossed into the bath-room.

"Where are you going?" Freddy asked.

"They gave me emergency leave. So I thought I would look around for a new reality, you know? Anyway, you could probably use your privacy."

Freddy nodded, unnerved by having solved another rid-dle. He grabbed his coat and headed right back out the door he had just come in.

Figs approached his house silently. Freddy was already in-side. Figs walked through the moonlight, standing in the middle of what used to be his living room. The roof of his house was burned away. The stars shown down into his kitchen and illuminated a charred silver toaster. Freddy was sitting in the middle of the burned place, fingering an equally charred device. He examined it with a flashlight that was browning out. He had been there for a while, crying.

"What's up?"

Figs turned, startled. He looked more mournful in this light, in this moment, than he had at either funeral.

"The lady cop—bomb squad, right?" Freddy said. "She sold you these caps and a timer."

Freddy wasn't asking questions. He held up a burned plastic device. Figs said nothing. He was busted. Only stu-pid people talked to cops. Figs listened to find out how much Freddy knew.

"Guess you figured with—Superboy—you figured you were covered. If you could just act like Marlon Brando and keep me busy—ol' Freddy, he would be too stupid to suspect anything."

Now Freddy had a question. He needed to understand

one thing about Figs. "You didn't know she was coming over that night, did you?"

Figs shook his head. He began to weep. The cop was finished as an actor. "She said she was going to her friend's—to watch pay per view. The thing—it was on a timer. I didn't know she would be here."

Figs pointed to the limp wooden tower. "She would be alive today if that bullshit tower still held water."

The tower excuse didn't hold water either.

"The Diagonal Rule is bullshit, Figs," Freddy said. He had decided by then that you followed the rule to *escape* a crime scene. Figs made rights at red lights to avoid detection. Call it the slow getaway.

Figs turned and wandered back toward his car, slumped and destroyed. Being found out by a friend was almost as bad as finding Monica dying on his lawn.

"Till you need it, Freddy, till you need it."

"I don't need traffic tips. *I need help.*"

But Figs kept walking to his car.

"I am gonna bring Superboy in and for once we are gonna tell the truth."

"You gotta find him first, before they do." Figs shook his head and opened the door to his car. He lit a cigarette and weighed his options. He stared at the great city across the way in the moonlight and then back at Freddy. The sheriff had never looked so alone.

Figs kicked a rock across the driveway.

"Freddy, I got—in my pocket—a check for two hundred grand. I got a chance to start my life again. I do not give a shit about this town or"—nodding at New York City—"that town or quote 'Justice,' unquote. Being right is not a bullet-proof vest."

Freddy said nothing, and a light flicked on in a neighbor's house. Figs got into the car, started it, and roared off to a new life. It seemed so easy.

Freddy watched him go and sighed. He looked out at the roof one last time and saw the abandoned water tower again. The faded GARRISON looked particularly huge, Freddy realized, when you were alone with it. Freddy squinted and rose. The shadows on the tower looked strange tonight. They flickered. Finally, the sheriff stood.

A field of reeds surrounded the base of the tower. There was a fresh path, trodden through the grass. Freddy began to climb the tower. The rusted ladder went on and on. Some of the metal rungs were broken. It took a lot of will and nerve to climb this high in the dark. The town lay quiet below him. Asleep. What was it they taught spies? Hide in plain sight.

The inside of the tower smelled of rust and chicken. When Murray Babitch opened his eyes, Freddy was standing right over him. Babitch was puffy-faced and unshaven, still wearing the blue plaid shirt he'd worn to his disappearing party. He had changed into sweatpants though. The wooden chamber was a mess—cans of Campbell's chicken and stars soup open, scattered all over the place.

Murray pointed a gun at the sheriff. Freddy wasn't impressed with guns anymore.

"Let's go," Freddy said.

Babitch closed his eyes, and considered escape. He lowered the gun. "Where?"

"I'm taking you to the city."

Babitch laughed. He made a wacky sound. They were a strange pair. About the same age, the same scars over their noses. Freddy was making sense of the situation, finally hearing the evidence. Babitch saved himself from capture and a watery grave by hiding in the driest place imaginable.

"Get dressed."

"Who are you working with, the Feds?"
Freddy shook his head.
"Internal Affairs?"
Freddy shook his head again.
"You're alone?"
Freddy nodded. He motioned to the clothes pile again.
"Just my luck."
"Get dressed."

Freddy had to climb down the tower first. It was an odd
capture. Only once he was down did Babitch come down.
The metal ladder could not have supported them both.
Freddy waited at the bottom rung with his gun out. When
Babitch reached the bottom, Freddy threw him a pair of
handcuffs.
"You know the routine," Freddy said.
As they passed through town, Babitch stared at the
cuffs. It was the ultimate violation for a cop. Most of the
guys who were arrested by IAD just had a simple request.
They didn't want to be paraded in front of the cameras in
cuffs. As they rolled along Main Street, Freddy stiffened.
Babitch, in the backseat, was jolted by the sight too.
"Oh, Christ," Babitch said.
Ray Donlan's Olds was parked outside the Four Aces
Tavern. Men milled about, waiting to get inside.
"Get down."
Even before he said it, Babitch was on the floor. He came
to town the same way he was leaving.
Freddy picked up his radio, and said, "Bill, you copy?"
There was no response. Freddy snapped off his lights.
"Bill, you out there?" Still no answer. He pulled into the
back of the station. No one saw them as they entered the
building. Freddy had never seen such a willing prisoner as
Babitch.

The lights in the office were out. Freddy did not turn them on. He escorted Babitch back to the cell, where he flopped down on the bench. And for a moment, Babitch wondered if he would be pulled from his cell by the town citizenry and lynched.

"You don't know what you're doing, do you?" Babitch said.

"Shut up."

Freddy walked over to the dispatch radio and flicked it on. For a dead guy, Babitch had a lot to say, Freddy thought, all of it annoying.

"Bill . . . You copy . . . Bill?"

Still no answer. It was 2:30 A.M., just about the last-call hour. Freddy walked to the window. Everyone in town, he could see, was in the bar. A Garrison patrol car was parked on the corner, too.

"Shit."

Freddy turned slightly and met Liz Randone's eyes. She studied him from the newspaper clip. The article was lit by the streetlamp. In that light, her crown looked lovely. Freddy walked across the room and picked up a set of keys on the desk. He moved to the door.

"Hey," Babitch said. "Wait a second. You can't leave me alone here."

Freddy turned back to his prisoner at the door and put a finger to his lips.

The prisoner fell silent.

THIRTY-TWO

If he were a fighter, Freddy would be a knockout waiting to happen. He was not a natural cop. His skills of detection were crude. He had known that over the last few weeks. And yet, there was no quit in Freddy Heflin. He would not run and hide. He did not take this job or live his life to do that. He was unsure of how it would end. But he understood nobility and fear. And now, again, Freddy was not afraid of what could happen to him.

These guys, he reasoned, made being a real cop easy. You did not have to carry the NYPD tin to know good from evil. Freddy Heflin, city wannabe, had never recognized true wickedness before. But now he was surrounded by profane and dangerous men living grotesque lives in a coarse, make-believe hamlet. It was curious, but in all of his ten years as the Garrison sheriff, Freddy had never truly understood, or appreciated, the responsibility of following the police canons of duty, service, and honor until this night. He dove into the bubbles again. Only this time Freddy Heflin was emerging from the slimy muck that was his town as the only true cop in Garrison, New Jersey.

Freddy wasn't sure how to play this. He hoped that decency and honor would matter to Ray Donlan. So, gun at his side, Freddy Heflin walked slowly and steadily down the middle of the street, headed for the Four Aces Tavern. Freddy may have been naive, but he believed in the inherent nature of men to do good. If reason failed, he always had the gun. But the old fullback would not be intimidated. Or at least he hoped not. He lit a cigarette to calm his nerves. He looked about, taking the town in as the bank clock moved. Freddy even imagined that he heard the tick of the clock.

The Garrison regulars were in the Four Aces. Bill was drinking with a couple of cops at the bar. They were on the sheriff's left as Freddy entered. Ray Donlan and the others were seated at the back of the bar at a couple of tables. Freddy focused on them as he came through the door. All conversation ended as Freddy entered the bar. The deputy turned and saw him.

"Just having a club soda," Bill explained.

"Finish it."

The sheriff continued to stride to the back table. Bill stood, and followed Freddy, a step behind. He was scared and reluctant. The deputy hadn't bargained for this when he'd signed on. Ray Donlan turned and saw Freddy come in. He swallowed his surprise and sat up. A version of the town clock was ticking in his head, too. The union had a gun to his head. And so did the mob. If the cops folded, and Garrison folded under the weight of Murray Babitch, so would all the bank mortgages in town. Mob collectors tended to be even more unforgiving, and lethal, than cops. They were all taking a chance on dying here.

"Hey, Freddy," he said, smiling.

"Hey, Ray. I came here to get Bill and Cindy, and I came to tell you—I found Superboy."

The smile on Donlan's face collapsed to the floor. Freddy found his voice as he continued.

"I'm bringing him in. Tomorrow morning. And I want you to come with me. I owe you that much."

"Uh-huh," Donlan said. He was seething, but controlled his rage. Freddy's eyes measured the room for danger. Cindy was sitting at a table behind Donlan, with Rucker. They seemed to be on some sort of half-assed date. Cindy would not look at him. Lagonda and Crasky sat at the table across from Donlan.

"He's a fugitive, Ray," Freddy continued. "And he's convinced you're going to kill him."

"He's a mixed-up kid. So are you."

"There has got to be a way out of this—for everyone. So I say we all go in tomorrow. Together. As a community of law-enforcement officers. And we unravel this. With lawyers or whatever. Together. Legal. In the city."

This petition was met with some laughter. Donlan was getting weary of this. The clock was ticking louder.

"Just tell me where he is, Freddy," Donlan said. "You got him in the station?"

A couple of cops shifted awkwardly with the weight of this confrontation. They had never heard Donlan talk openly like this. He reeked of desperation. Freddy's Boy Scout routine and searching eyes made them equally uneasy. Freddy was in over his head. He wiped the sweat from his brow but remained standing. Bill and Cindy studied him, measuring his commitment to this confrontation.

"Listen to me, Freddy," Ray said.

He was turned all the way around. Freddy stood with his back to the door. Bill had his back. But some cops were moving away from him, not toward him. They whispered to each other like partners in a poker game, their faces asking, "Are we in?"

"Do you know the difference between men and boys? Boys bet *everything* on *everything*. Boys think every hand is a royal flush. You play cards with a man, he knows his limits. He thinks of his family—back home—before he bets the house and the car."

"Ray—" Freddy said.

"Listen to the man, Freddy," Leo Crasky, the precinct broom turned detective, demanded. They were a table of warm beer and snarls.

"Freddy, I invited cops—*men, good men*—to live here, in this town. And these men, to make a living, they cross that bridge *every day,* to a place where *everything* is upside down, where the *cop* is the perp and the perp is the *victim.* But they play by the rules. They keep their guns in their holsters and they play by the rules. The only thing they ever did was get their families out—before it got to them."

The bar belonged to him, too. The cops were nodding in agreement with his soliloquy. Some of them even *believed* what Ray Donlan was saying.

"We built homes—across the river—we made a place where things make sense and you can walk across the street without fear."

More nods all around. Freddy had listened to enough operas and classical music to recognize a crescendo when it was coming.

"And tonight—you come to me, your body pumping with adrenaline—you found my nephew, you feel powerful with your accomplishment, so you come to me with a plan. A plan to set things right, everyone in the city holding hands, singing 'We Are the World.' It's very nice."

The cops laughed at Donlan's joke.

"It's a nice plan. But, Freddy, your plan is the plan of a boy. You made it on the back of a matchbook—without thinking—*without looking at the cards.* I look at the cards and I see Superboy crucified. I see this town destroyed. That's not what you want, is it?"

Freddy spoke in a low, almost groaning, voice.

"Ray, I look at this town—and I don't like what I see anymore."

The cops at Donlan's table groaned. Rucker moved closer to Freddy, to the end of his table. Cindy was magnetized, but still uncommitted.

"What does that mean?"

"There is something sick about this town."

Donlan was aghast. The thing was burning down in front of him. "Who the fuck do you think you are?"

Freddy put his hands on his hips, and shifted his belt before answering. "I am the sheriff of Garrison, New Jersey."

"Then be the sheriff," Donlan barked. "Protect this town. Defend these men."

The amazing thing about all this was that the killers had talked themselves into believing they were the victims. In this gathering, Donlan's homily of lies passed for gospel. The bar, and the bigger town, simmered with imagined injustice. Lagonda, who sat at the table like a mountain of suet, finally exploded.

"The grass hasn't even taken root above Joey's grave, you fuck," he said.

Rucker went him one further. He placed his gun on the table and played with it. Freddy weighed the psychotic cop closely.

"You feel like a cop now, Freddy, sticking it inside a cop's widow?"

Freddy recoiled from the lie, but would not address Rucker. Some of the other cops were getting uncomfortable. They reasoned that Donlan was making a toddler's bet in this game. Ray cursed Rucker. A few of the cops left.

"I'm outta here, Ray," one said, passing the table.

"Too rich for me," said another.

Cindy and Bill were frozen. They were equally torn, unsure just how far they were willing to back Freddy up in a dispute with the town. As Freddy studied Rucker, his hand touched his holster. Cindy looked away.

"Freddy," Donlan asked again. "Have you got him at the station?"

Freddy said nothing. Everyone in the room, except Cindy and Bill, wanted to know.

"Just drop the keys. Maybe they fell out of your pocket. Or maybe Cindy's. And you go home and you sleep. And you wake up tomorrow, and you guide that traffic through town . . ."

There were tears in Freddy's eyes. Not because of the unspeakable fear he felt but because of the decision he had made, the man he had just become. Figs was right. Being a cop was being a lonely, tortured, piece of shit. And Freddy Heflin was a cop now.

"And everything will be the same," Donlan finished. "It will be the way it was."

Freddy looked at the clock on the wall. There was no time in his life for cowardice anymore. He had already made his decision. He would matter. Not for the good of himself, but for the good of the just and the moral.

"Uh, I'm leaving at six. That's in a few hours. I'd like for you to come with me, Ray."

Bill joined Freddy, hesitant. Donlan wilted. This was becoming too much waste to clean up.

"There is nothing I can say?"

Freddy's solemn face said Donlan should be finished. The lieutenant threw up his hands. To the end, Ray Donlan was being the controlled, reasonable man. But this, too, was all act and craftiness. Rucker still hadn't holstered his gun.

"Okay, then," Donlan said. "Six it is. It's a date."

Freddy blinked, stunned with Donlan's answer and his

own performance. Fortune did seem to favor the daring. At the very least, Freddy had delivered a gutty performance.

"Okay. I'll see you then."

Freddy shuffled uneasily back out the door. It was the toughest ten yards he had ever covered. Bill, the harmless man, followed, trying to look as tough as Freddy had just sounded. Freddy looked to Cindy as he backpedaled. She was looking at Rucker, measuring his madness against her scorn. She shook her head, tearful with indecision. Freddy pulled the door closed.

THIRTY-THREE

Murray Babitch paced in his cell, certain he was going to *really* die tonight. There was a good chance he was right. This was as hairy as any situation he had ever survived in Brooklyn. At least he'd been armed there. Handcuffs drove him crazy. Once he'd been sitting in the front seat with his partner, Mark Klobes, driving a handcuffed prisoner to central booking. The guy wasn't even their prisoner, for Chrissakes. They'd picked him up after he'd robbed a store on Nostrand Avenue in east Flatbush. Very tame stuff. They were about six blocks into the trip along Eastern Parkway when the guy pulled a second gun from the small of his back and hit Mark Klobes with a single head shot from the backseat. Mark had died instantly. They had never patted the guy down for a second gun. He'd tried to shoot Murray Babitch, too, but he couldn't swing around to shoot anyone on the left side of the car fast enough. He scrambled out of the car and Superboy shot the guy twelve times as he tried to run away from the car. The department gave him a medal. He left it on the grave of Mark Klobes.

"At least give me a gun so I can help defend myself when they come to hang me from the lamppost," Babitch said. "You guys have never even fired guns in anger. We are all gonna die."

That was an option, sure. The room told you that. There

were two shotguns on the table. Freddy sat, slumped, facing the window. Bill paced, but on a short cable leash, attached to the phone. A single firebomb, shattering through the window, would have killed them.

"No, honey," Bill Geisler told his wife over the phone. "I'm telling you because I just can't leave him."

There was no place to hide, and everyone knew that. Freddy might have called the county sheriff, or the state police for backup, but there was no telling who Ray Donlan knew, or where, well enough to put one shot behind your ear. To call anyone for help now, Freddy reasoned, was to take a chance on dying. And he wasn't sophisticated enough to call any media types. This arrangement was chance enough. Ray was going to come, but not to surrender, and not unarmed. Unlike the Old West, high noon arrived at dawn in Cop Land.

Bill hung up the phone. Slowly. He was extremely frightened. This wasn't chance. This wasn't some maniac jumping out of a vehicle on a routine car stop with both guns blazing. A careful cop could protect himself from dying that easily. But this was lunacy. Freddy had invited Ray Donlan, and Jack Rucker, to kill them. The clock kept moving, even though the second hand was stuck. It was four-thirty. There was a car outside, just idle and waiting.

"Go home, Bill," Freddy said.

"I mean, Freddy, I want to be here for you. But . . . Lisa is nervous. I didn't tell you till now, but she's pregnant. I mean, there's a reason I never applied for the city job. I didn't want that *danger*. This is your thing."

Bill wasn't a willful coward, or even an absent one. He was just genuinely tortured, although Babitch, who was grumbling in the background, didn't sound to Freddy like he saw it that way.

"So, go on," Freddy said. "I'm gonna be fine." He even

managed a smile as he dismissed his only backup. "They're not going to kill me."

Babitch disagreed, and said so.

"Why don't you just go now?"

"I told him I was leaving at six," Freddy said. "Besides, they're out there already."

Bill nodded, then said, "Take care, Freddy."

Freddy nodded, and tried to not to show how spent he was. But Bill could see the exhaustion. On his way out the door, Bill passed the old clipping about a young man's rescue of a young woman. Babitch put his equally tortured head in his hands.

About an hour south of the station, on the deserted Jersey Turnpike, Figs barreled on to freedom, the green check hot in his back pocket. The car was piled with his belongings. Police Officer Gary Figgis was whacked out, by any definition of the phrase. But he was not high. At least not yet. He kept staring at himself in the rearview mirror as he drove. He was alone in the car, and running. And Figs did not like the company.

"Shut the fuck up, would you please," he said, staring at himself.

Figs looked once more, then hit the brakes. This was not Monica sitting, unknowing, in a building with a firebomb. This was Freddy being left behind in a town with another ticking bomb. The Chevy screeched to a stop on the deserted highway.

As the sun rose over the distant city, birds began to sing outside the sheriff's office. It was just a few minutes before six. Freddy awoke with a start, and looked out the window. The street was empty, even desolate. The car parked out in front the previous night was gone. The commuters would be taking shortcuts through town in another hour. The school busses would be warm and ready to go in thirty minutes. Was it time to die?

"Oh, well."

Freddy took a shotgun from the desk and opened Babitch's cell. He was sitting there, groggy.

"Come on. We're going."

THIRTY-FOUR

They came out the front door a moment later, the morning sun a mud yellow. It lit the way as they rounded the corner and walked through an alley behind the sheriff's office. Freddy's dented car was parked there. Freddy stopped in his tracks. All four of his tires had been slashed.

"Oh, God," Babitch said. He had seen enough deflated and blown-out tires to last a lifetime. A night in the old tire storage turned holding cell hadn't impaired his memory.

A hand reached from behind Freddy and took his shotgun. The sheriff felt the cold press of steel against his head. And he was afraid.

"Get down." Jack Rucker pushed Freddy to his knees. Lagonda grabbed Babitch. Rucker pushed Freddy's back. "I said, get down, Freddy."

There was no color in Freddy's face. He wasn't sure how this would go, but he hadn't expected to die, well, so easily. He was down on all fours; he was going to die like some damaged dog.

"Jesus, guys. You don't want to do this," Freddy said.

Oh, but they did. Jack Rucker wanted to do this kind of thing every night of his life. And on many nights he had.

"Don't shit in your pants, Freddy, we ain't gonna kill you." Rucker touched the muzzle of his gun to Freddy's left ear. "This is the good one, right?"

Freddy nodded. He closed his eyes as he heard the tumbler click. He heard the hammer pull, too.

Crack!

The gun fired a round. But it didn't fly into Freddy's skull, or split his brain. It went right into the pavement. Freddy did not realize that in the first searing moments of pain. He thought he was dead.

But Rucker had fired the gun into the ground. Freddy rolled on the pavement, powder burns covering his left ear and blood trickling out of it. The gun blast had the desired effect—it deafened him. If Rucker had fired a simple BB into his eardrum it could not have done more damage. The sheriff was now completely deaf.

Frantic with pain, he rolled over again, watching as Rucker and Lagonda loaded Babitch into their car. They roared up the road, toward the housing tracts on the hill, leaving Freddy alone and deaf on the roadside. He struggled to stand, but his equilibrium was gone, too. He collapsed to his knees and tried to remember what a song sounded like.

The silence was constant and unnerving. Freddy invented a rumbling piano to cover his terror. He was still on his knees, the blood trickling out of his ear. It was a good move, typical Jack Rucker. He shook his head and tried to focus on Ray Donlan. *Got to get him.*

At a neatly kept house across the street, a cop came out on the steps in his bathrobe and retrieved the morning paper. He was not deaf, and had certainly heard the gunshot. And yet he did not seem to see Freddy, standing now and stumbling up the center of the road. The blood was running, leaking out of the sheriff's left ear and running down his neck and soaking his shirt. His face was pale, draining by the second.

Freddy Heflin had a revolver in one hand and a shotgun

in the other. His badge glinted against the dawn. And still, he trudged through the maddening silence. His face was stone. So was the face of the cop watching this spectacle from the front porch of his home. Their eyes met. The cop turned around and closed his door.

Freddy marched on. He trudged up a steep hill and past the mailbox that read RANDONE. Freddy could hear music in both ears, a wild piano being pounded. Or maybe that was his beating heart. For Freddy, all sounds were imagined.

He was deaf to the barking Randone Doberman, pulling at his chain. Freddy saw the silent bark, and moved on. He was focused on what was ahead.

Liz Randone looked out her bedroom window and saw him, dazed and bloody, moving toward the Donlans's street. In the distance, at Donlan's house, Rucker, Lagonda, and Crasky stood on the stoop. They held guns at their sides. Freddy could see that. He moved forward with silent desperation. They were alerted by the bark of the dogs and the screams of neighbors Freddy could not hear. Freddy alone heard evil in Garrison, and he trooped forward into the silent abyss.

The piano in his head was furious, and distant. He kept marching into the sound. In the background, Liz Randone screamed. She was on her front lawn, desperately yelling to a man who could no longer hear. Unhearing, Freddy kept walking. For over twenty years, Liz had never heard him either.

Donlan emerged from his house, his arm around Babitch. Technically, it was time to die.

Lagonda turned, seeing Freddy first. He shouted to Donlan and the others. Donlan turned, stunned with the spirit of the trudging, bloodied policeman and his own underestimation of the man.

Freddy was in full stride now, moving toward the house.

Neighbors slammed doors on him. He blinked and wiped the blood from his ear.

Jack Rucker pointed a finger at Freddy, saying something, screaming a barrage of unheard insults and warnings at the sheriff. Lagonda pointed his gun at Freddy and shouted something. Donlan and Crasky soundlessly pulled Babitch, kicking and screaming, back into the house.

The music only Freddy could hear was steady.

Freddy saw the muzzle of Lagonda's gun flare. The windshield of a car silently shattered. Freddy did not even blink. The silence made him bulletproof. The shot, without the attendant fury of sound, seemed harmless.

Liz heard the screams and the shot. She ran back to her door. Freddy raised his own gun, then fired. But there was no sound. Lagonda crumpled to the ground, clutching his shattered leg. Rucker roared again, then raised his gun. But this time the target shot back. Freddy wasn't hanging, helpless, on a wire in an amusement park for cops anymore.

Freddy and Rucker fired at the same time. The muzzles flared. Rucker fell backward onto pavement. The bullet had hit him in the chest and his gun flew away. Then Police Officer Jack Rucker, the loud man, was finally quiet.

But Freddy stood, unscathed. Again, he walked steadily toward the front door of the house. Rucker and Lagonda were lying on the ground beneath him. They were both bloody. Rucker's eyes were wet and red. He shouted curses against his fear. But with no other cop on his wooded street, no one heard his cries of collapse.

Leo Crasky peered around the house. He had grabbed one of Joey Randone's hunting rifles off the wall inside the house. Now he pointed the shotgun at Freddy. From behind him, Liz screamed an unheard warning. Freddy, oblivious to the threat and the sound, continued to move toward the front door. Crasky fired. Suddenly, there was a spray of blood across the front door. Confused, Freddy touched his shoulder. He had been hit.

Crasky stood at the side of the house, the shotgun smoking in his hands. He raised it again to fire at Freddy. Suddenly, a silent blast ripped through Crasky's torso. His own gun fell, firing helplessly into the air. He fell backward, slack.

Freddy turned slightly and discovered Figs standing in the middle of the street, cordite still smoking from his raised revolver.

Lying on his back, Lagonda fired a wild shot at Freddy Heflin, but missed. Freddy hammered a single shot into Lagonda's abundant body. In death, there was a beached, gasping, whale quality to the loathsome detective. From the street behind Freddy, Figs saw that, and more. Just then, he screamed, and ran forward.

Ray Donlan fired a single shot at Freddy from his front door.

It was actually quite hard to hit a moving target. Every cop knew that. Donlan's shot skittered off cars down the block. Freddy did not hear the shot, but he did see the lieutenant who had hung his own partner, Glenn Tunney, from his jail cell.

Freddy fired into the door, as did Figs, and the wood splintered. Donlan retreated into his house.

Freddy followed, bloody and quiet. He just followed the music deeper into the piano. He saw blood on the carpet. He moved down the hallway that was the museum of Ray Donlan's police life. The walls were decorated with medals, citations of heroism, headlines and photos. Freddy did not live on the wall. He wasn't good enough to exist as either a memory or a cop in Ray Donlan's house. He moved slowly, both hands on his pistol. Below the scrapbook, there was blood smeared along the wall of union heroes. Donlan was hit. The blood on the cream carpet led up the stairs.

Freddy climbed the stairs. His eyes searched frantically. He was wild with the silence now, completely unprotected. He might have waited for Figs, but Freddy was done with waiting. He could have waited, too, by the side of the water for help, all those years ago. Freddy was deaf to waiting, too. Figs entered the house below him, and shouted up. Freddy rounded the banister and pushed open the bedroom door. He trained his gun on the middle of the room. This view revealed Rose Donlan, huddled on the bed. Babitch was at the window. He had a leg sticking out and was trying to get onto the roof. There was a frozen, gaping moment. Rose and Babitch started at Freddy. And past him. Freddy's eyes followed them. He saw a more severe blood trail on the carpet. The track loped around the room. Toward the bed and back around. It ended where Freddy stood, at the door.

Donlan, severely wounded already, now heard the silence of the tracker and understood. Freddy spun and fired. Donlan leaped from his hiding spot behind the door. Freddy's bullet tore into his gut. Donlan fell, contorted, spewing silent screams at the sheriff's feet.

"I can't hear you, Ray," Freddy said.

The sheriff couldn't hear himself either. As Donlan crumpled, and the town crumbled, Figs arrived at his new partner's side.

In the golden light of morning, blood and death on Ray Donlan's block seemed as impossible as a town built for cops. The cops stood around in robes and sweatpants, studying the stained terrain. Their families watched from behind doors and windows. They were in awe. Most cops come and go through their police career without ever firing their guns, even in New York City. Still, Freddy Heflin, they all saw, was as big as anyone they had ever worked with.

They stood back on the sidewalk to make room for *their* sheriff. Cindy Betts was on the radio in her patrol car, requesting help from the state police as Bill tended to the wounded. They both looked up, dull-faced and astounded. Freddy and Figs emerged with Babitch.

Liz stood on the corner. Her eyes met Freddy's as he dragged Babitch past Cindy and to a patrol car. Liz took a step backward.

Every hero's work was a series of choices.

THIRTY-FIVE

They were on the George Washington Bridge again. The cops were taking their prisoner into the city. Rush-hour traffic had never looked so good to Murray Babitch. He wanted to be careful to point out the spot where he'd shot the kids, and the point on the great gray monstrosity where he'd disappeared, too.

"I died right there," Babitch wanted to say. But he said nothing, numb with Freddy's last stand.

"The crazy fuck," Babitch muttered.

Freddy was driving silently, a pool of blood welling on his lap from the wound on his shoulder. Figs ripped the sheriff's shirt and tied the wound off with a tourniquet. Babitch was in the backseat, babbling.

"He's deaf," Babitch said. "They shot out his ears, man."

Freddy pulled to a stop at the toll booth, then handed the toll taker three bucks. She was nonchalant. From her seat, she had seen worse, much worse. Especially on the overnight shift, coming the other way. Some people would do anything to beat the toll.

"It's four dollars," she said.

"Huh?" Freddy said. Total deafness was constant confusion.

Figs handed Freddy another single. "FREDDY. HERE. IT'S FOUR NOW."

Freddy pulled his car through the gate and onto the bridge. Figs shook his head in wonder.

"He's been watching too much *Gunsmoke,*" Babitch said. "He's crazy. He is. He is fucking nuts."

Figs turned and met Babitch's eyes. Then he smiled with derangement. "No," Figs said. "He's a cop."

Then he laughed out loud and said, "Hey, Superboy, show me the red light where you made the hard right turn . . . off the bridge."

Freddy just continued across the bridge, proud and oblivious. He glanced at Figs as they crossed the line on the bridge that said they were in New York City. Figs put a spinning red light on the dashboard. He didn't bother with the siren. Freddie wouldn't have appreciated a good police wail right now, anyway.

After they hurtled down the West Side Highway, and tried to spot Garrison from the opposite shore, Freddy turned his car down Chambers Street and lurched over a curb near Manhattan Borough Hall. He just parked the car there. The sight of it angered some citizens heading into the parking violations bureau to pay their overdue parking tickets. One Police Plaza rose above them.

Babitch, his hands in handcuffs, bucked. The car was surrounded by cops. He knew some of their faces.

"Hey, it's Bobby Doyle," Babitch said.

The cops were all around the car, eating food from the stands in the plaza. They were a sea of Danish pastries, pretzels, souvlaki, and hot dogs. They stared into the car at its grim occupants. Freddy got out of the car in his bloody, sopping shirt.

"You can't park there buddy," one cop said. "Hey."

Oblivious, Freddy dragged Babitch behind him in handcuffs. Some of the cops recognized him from the front page of the newspaper. A couple of guys in the plaza had attended his funeral. Figs climbed out and tried to help. Freddy shook him off.

Moe Tilden, on his lunch break with the rest of the cops from police headquarters, walked from a hot dog stand. He was biting into the hot dog when he recognized the men. "Holy shit," he said.

Freddy looked up, still dazed.

"Hey," Babitch yelled at a cop he recognized from the academy. "Hey, Bobby."

The cop looked at him. And then down at the handcuffs. "Hey, Soups," the cop said. "What the fuck? Thought you were dead. What the hell is going on?"

"Crazy shit," Babitch said.

Freddy pulled Babitch along. They had about twenty yards to go to the lobby. Figs pulled out his shield.

"We're cool, boys. We're cool."

Freddy faced a blue wall of cops. They stood, frozen against him.

"Please move," Freddy said.

They turned to stone. They were a ring of blue hatred.

Freddy searched the plaza. His weary eyes caught Tilden through the crowd.

"Get away from him," the Internal Affairs lieutenant yelled. "Hey, back off."

Carson and the other snoops from the unit held up their badges. "It's cool. It's cool."

Freddy struggled to bring Babitch into view of Tilden. He nearly collapsed on the pavement. He needed to hold his prisoner for support. The police barricade was silent and steady and confused.

"Call EMS," Tilden yelled.

Carson nodded and disappeared into the building. Tilden turned toward Freddy. Freddy blinked. He was anesthetized and bloody. The men weighed the cop in him.

Tilden felt all their eyes on his back. He took Babitch by the other shoulder, then turned to face Freddy. Moe Tilden was a pair of green eyes blazing through the blue world.

Freddy looked up at him. The sheriff was weary but proud.

Tilden gestured toward the door of One Police Plaza with a cock of his head. "Come on inside."

They walked in together, slowly and proudly, through the glass doors of One Police Plaza—as cop partners did throughout the city and country—reporting for police duty.

Mike McAlary was nominated for a Pulitzer Prize for his coverage of New York's 77th precinct scandal, the topic of his best-seller *Buddy Boys*. He is also the author of *Cop Shot* and *Good Cop, Bad Cop*. He has been a columnist for the *New York Post* and currently writes for the New York *Daily News*.